THE DEVIL MAY CARE

HELL'S ANGEL BOOK ONE

JANE HINCHEY

BAYWOLF PRESS

BP

BAYWOLF PRESS

AUTHOR'S NOTE

Dear Reader,

Big news in my literary world! As you know, I've been writing as both Jane Hinchey and Zahra Stone. It's been quite the adventure, but now it's time for a change. I'm bringing everything back under my original name, Jane Hinchey. Just like my stories, life has its twists, and this is the latest one for me.

What does this mean for your Zahra Stone favorites? They're getting a fresh look with my real name, but the stories inside are the same ones you love.

As you delve into The Devil May Care, you're not just reading a story, but joining me on my author's journey. Your support has been invaluable, and I'm so grateful for it.

Here's to more mystery, more romance, and more adventures together!

xoxo

Jane

Think your job's bad? Mine's Hell. *Literally.*

Hi, I'm Lucy AKA Lucifer, and I'm the CEO of Hell. It's my job to mete out justice in the afterlife, to serve as warden for sinful souls until their sentences are served so they can cross through those pearly gates in the sky and I never have to see their sorry faces again.

Most of the time, it's actually a pretty easy gig.

But some idiot humans—playing with a Ouija board of all things—just opened an interdimensional portal on earth, and somehow it falls to me to stop the terrible monster now running amok as it feasts on the souls of humans.

So now I'm on earth, trying my best to blend in while also attempting to catch this thing before it destroys humanity for good. And the more time I spend with one human in particular, the more I kind of don't want to go back to my old 9-to-5…

"What do you mean, a breach?" I glanced at Ashliel over my shoulder. Her long red hair with tendrils of dancing flames flowed over her shoulders. I sighed. I loved her hair. My own jet-black locks refused to take the flame. My wings, on the other hand? They were magnificent.

"Um. A hole?" Ashliel suggested tentatively.

We were in the pit, well, not literally *in* the pit—that was for sinners, and I was not one. I had a progress report to prepare and wanted to make sure everything was in tip-top shape. Only now, Ashliel, my wonderful, super-efficient assistant, was telling me someone had punched a hole in Earth's dimension.

"How did this happen?" I asked. "There are protocols in place. Safeguards. Who could punch a hole in Earth's dimension, and what would the purpose be?" Spinning on my Gucci heel, I strode from the pit, ignoring the wailing from below. Ashliel had sucked all the fun out of my inspection.

Hurrying after me, she spoke up. "To let something in, I'd assume."

A chill ran through me. Not something. Someone. To let someone in was much more likely. Heaven, Hell, and Earth were closely linked, and while I wasn't responsible for Earth, I monitored what was happening in that realm. I'd been running Hell for all of eternity. I'd built it to what it was today. A well-oiled machine. Punishment befitting your sins was dished out. Once done, you got to ascend to Heaven. Of course, most sinners who found themselves here, well, let's just say their sins were so deep, dark, and wicked they had no chance of leaving Hell. Ever. They were my eternal guests.

A smile danced across my red lips. I loved my job. Took great pride in it. Although I'd sent in progress reports every few hundred years as requested, I had yet to hear from Father. God. The creator. I assumed all was well. He would not be pleased to hear of this breach. Nor was I, for that matter. Not that it was technically my problem. The breach had been on Earth, not here. Only I had to make sure it wasn't someone from Hell trying to get back to Earth. It had never happened before; security was too tight, but there was always a first time.

"I want a head count. Every soul in this place needs to be accounted for. The breach had better not have come from here!" Striding across the walkway suspended over the pit, Ashliel's heels clipping along behind me to keep pace, I headed for the glass elevator in the cliff face. I needed to get to my office and get this shit storm sorted, pronto.

"Ummm. Lucy?" Ashliel stepped in beside me, electronic clipboard in hand.

"Yes, Ash?" I knew she had a long list of requests, meetings, messages. As CEO of Hell, my days were busy. I'd built my torturous dimension to great heights over the last few hundred millennia. In the previous two hundred years alone, attendance of lost souls entering Hell had risen over two hundred percent. That number looked to be on the rise.

"There's a man who wants his punishment of having a buzzard constantly pecking his eyes out to be lessened, a man whose memories have been wiped and he wants to know who he was, and a woman who wants to warn her sister on Earth about the afterlife." She spoke fast, knowing my time was limited.

"Buzzard man, no can do. This isn't a negotiation. His punishment was set when he entered Hell. He knows this. Deny future requests. Memory man...good point, how can he atone for his sins if he can't remember them? See to it that his sinful memories are returned. Only his sins, mind you. And no to the woman who wants to warn her sister—they get plenty of warnings. It's not like this place is a secret."

Ashliel's fingers flew across her clipboard. By the time we reached my office, she was done. Before stepping out of the glass box, I looked down into the fiery pit where the most heinous sinners resided. It was eerily beautiful from this vantage point. Sighing, I turned my back on the bubbling pit of fire and exited the elevator, stepping into the opulence of Hell HQ.

I greatly admired the skyscrapers on Earth and had modeled Hell HQ on them. Over two hundred floors, soaring high into the red and orange sky, built from gleaming black marble. My offices took up ten floors alone; the very top floor was my penthouse. Yes, I lived in luxury, but I damn well earned it. Running Hell was hard work, never a moment's peace. And now this. A breach. It niggled me. Security was tight. It couldn't have come from the pit; I was just there. Had it come from one of the cell blocks housed on the other side of Hell HQ?

I crossed to the floor-to-ceiling windows and looked out on the cells. Row upon row of fifty-story skyscrapers, all housing sinners. They spanned as far as the eye could see, each one providing different levels of punishment. Wingless Demons patrolled the streets, their black skin and red eyes clearly identifying them. Their winged counterparts took to the skies, massive wings spanning over twenty feet, soaring around and around the buildings. Who could escape this? That is, if the breach had even come from Hell in the first place. Earth was my brothers' responsibility. They were charged with watching over the humans. I was annoyed I was being dragged into it, yet I liked the humans. I didn't want to see them destroyed by some other dimension creature. Not if I could stop it.

A ding on Ashliel's clipboard caught my attention. I arched a dark brow at her.

"You have a delivery."

"Probably from my brothers." I sighed. Had they heard the news and were already poking fun?

"They might have sent something nice," Ashliel suggested, ever hopeful.

"Knowing my brothers, I doubt it."

Stepping through the glass doors into my office, I spied a huge gift-wrapped parcel on my sleek black desk. Here we go.

"Thank you, Ashliel. That will be all." I waited for Ash to leave the room, then approached my desk cautiously. What were they up to? Gabriel and Michael were archangels like me, but when Father chose me over them to head up the Hell Division, to say the boys were a little prickly was an understatement. We hadn't spoken in over a hundred years. Why now? Today? Were they connected to the breach? Did they instigate it? I wouldn't put it past them. They'd do anything to see me fail.

Hoping I was wrong and that maybe, just maybe, the box on my desk was an olive branch, I tore open the wrapping and cautiously opened the lid. Inside was a single piece of paper. On it was written the name, "Emily Barlow." Who the Hell was Emily Barlow? Was she a lost soul? I reached to pull the paper from the box, but the whole thing went up in flames. *Great.*

With a wave of my hand, I put out the flames

and cleaned the debris from my desk before crossing to the giant screen across the room, one so big that I had to stand in front of it, or if I preferred, recline on the leather couch a few feet away. I could split the screen into hundreds of smaller screens and monitor Earth and Hell at the same time if I so chose. This time I raised my hand and halved the screen, keeping an eye on my own dimension on the left and scanning through files searching for Emily Barlow on the right. There were several humans with that name, and I flicked through until one caught my eye.

There. Emily Barlow. Human. Alive. Her dossier flashed across the screen, a mini-movie of her life so far. She was young, a teenager, seventeen, a high school student, blonde hair, blue eyes, pretty. She was a bossy little thing and liked to be involved in community events and social activities. She wanted a career in Public Relations or the Media. As I watched, the screen glitched, froze, then resumed. Emily was in a graveyard. Something was there with her. Something dark. I leaned forward, watching intently as Emily was clasped in a tight embrace, held for a matter of seconds, then let go. Glowing red eyes looked up directly at me. Then it was gone, leaving Emily's body on the ground, drained of life.

The screen flickered, a brief moment of static,

before settling again. This time I no longer saw Emily but a man. He was sitting at a table, one hand resting on the table, palm up, and in the center of his palm a deep azure blue rock. He sent the message. Did he mean to send it to me, I wonder? His eyes sprang open, and he flopped back in his seat as if exhausted. I looked into his eyes, magnified the screen, so it focused on his face. A very handsome face: strong jaw covered in a light beard, full lips that held my attention for slightly too long. I wondered what they looked like when he smiled.

Then I wondered...*why am I wondering about his lips? Okay, seriously, he's a human*, I scolded myself. But it had been a long time since I'd...you know. Had any fun in that department. Maybe a dalliance with a human would take my mind off the stresses of running Hell. As much as I loved my job, I'd yet to have a vacation. I shifted my attention from his kissable lips to his eyes. A combination of hazel and gold, they were striking with their dark lashes. And the way he was looking directly into the screen, it was as if he were looking right at me.

Decision made.

"Ashliel?" I called. "Hold down the fort. I'm going topside." I'd deal with the breach and spend some quality time with—

"Who's that?" Ashliel strode into my office, heels clipping across the floor and breaking into my thoughts.

"That is Levi Forrester, and he sent me a delivery I intend to collect personally." With a wink, I was gone.

TWO

I arrived on Earth with a flash of lightning, a clap of thunder, and a torrential downpour. I wished I could lay claim to the theatrics, but it was Mother Nature's doing, talented bitch that she was.

Blessed with night vision, I examined the cemetery I'd landed in, a very dark, very spooky cemetery in what appeared to be the middle of nowhere. The darkness was absolute, the heavy clouds blocking any illumination from the heavens.

The wind whipped around my legs, sending a shiver through me. It was so much hotter in Hell that Shadow Falls' spring chill, where I now found myself, took a bit of getting used to. With merely a thought, a long leather jacket materialized and wrapped itself around me, snuggly hugging my curves and flowing freely to my ankles, blocking the bite of the wind.

A tingle ran up my spine, reminding me of why I was here. Levi had sent me his vision of Emily being killed, and now that I was here, I could feel it. It niggled at me like an irritating itch that you just couldn't reach. As much as the lure of finding Levi had me grinning in anticipation, the sense of something otherworldly had me frowning in concern. Whatever was here had no business being here.

I cast my eyes around the graveyard, searching. Then I found her. Lying in a puddle, her pale face turned toward me. Her white dress was plastered to her body, her eyes wide open, unseeing.

I knelt by her side, touched my fingers to her throat to be certain. As soon as my fingers landed on her icy cold skin, two things became apparent. One, she was dead. Two, her soul had been taken from her. Violently. I could see the tattered remains of it where it had been ripped from her.

Ignoring the cold, I knelt by her side, clasping her hand in mine, channeling her soul, attempting to follow its journey, but there was nothing, the tattered scraps that remained revealing no trace of what had happened here. They were enough to tell me she was an innocent, a good decent person. She wasn't slated for Hell. This girl had been Heaven bound...until someone stole her soul.

"FREEZE! Don't move. This is the police."

I closed my eyes with a sigh. The police. Of course it was. The law enforcement on Earth did their best, but when their own ranks were as corrupt as the sinners they tried to punish, it was an uphill battle. Despite the limitations placed on them, I applauded those who continued to believe and continued to protect the innocent.

A hand grabbed my upper arm and pulled me to my feet, pushing me none too gently against the tree looming over us. I winced as my cheek came into contact with the roughness of the bark. The same hands ran up and down my body, patting along my legs, waist, shoulders.

"Well, hello, Officer," I purred, turning my head to eye the tall man who was currently running his large hands over my body.

Satisfied I wasn't concealing any sort of weapon, he turned me around to face him. He was very nice to look at with his dark, brooding looks, chiseled jaw, enough of a five o'clock shadow to make me want to run my fingers across his jaw just for the buzz. I didn't pay much attention to the goings-on topside, but if all the men were this good-looking, I'd be visiting more often. His brow furrowed.

"It's detective. Not officer."

"Okay then."

"What's your name?"

"Lucifer. But my friends call me Lucy."

"Lucifer?" His brows rose in disbelief. "Your parents named you Lucifer?"

"Kinda. It's a long story."

"Lucifer who?"

"Just Lucifer."

"What are you doing here, Lucifer?" He didn't press me for a surname.

"I was sent a message to come here."

"A message? From who?"

Not wanting to get Levi in trouble with the cops, I amended my story, not a lie, since I can't lie, but I can avoid the truth. "It doesn't matter who it was from, just that a soul stealer has found its way to your realm. I followed the energy, and it led me here."

"Soul stealer? You followed the energy? What on earth are you talking about?" A woman stepped into view. I won't say she was hiding behind the detective, but...others may claim otherwise. She was dressed in jeans that looked to be a size too big for her, baggy in an unflattering way, a gray T-shirt that had seen better days judging by the stretched and frayed neckline, and a green waterproof jacket. Around her neck a chain with a police badge at the end of it. She had her gun drawn and aimed at me.

"Allow me to explain in small words so you'll understand." I aimed my words at her, for I'd already felt and filed away the vibe I was getting from the handsome detective in front of me. He was halfway on board with my story. This woman wasn't. "I am Lucifer. I rule Hell. I'm the CEO, if you will, and we had an alert that someone Earth side is up to no good, messing with dimensions that shouldn't be messed with. I popped up to check it out since it became apparent my brothers weren't going to, and that's when I discovered this poor girl, her soul stolen."

The woman scowled, then whipped a pair of handcuffs out. "Fucking fruitcakes," she grumbled.

I'D FORGOTTEN how touchy and sensitive humans could be. Sitting now in an interview room, my wrists in handcuffs and chained to the table in front of me, I held my temper. Just. Ashliel would laugh if she could see me now.

Oh, the handcuffs and chains weren't an issue—human restraints couldn't actually restrain me. Still, I let the detectives believe they could. I could have left this place with a flick of my wings, but I needed to find out what the police knew. They'd introduced themselves as Detective Jared Morrison and Detective Nicole James. He referred to her as Nic, and I got the feeling they'd been working together for a long time. I didn't miss the puppy dog eyes she gave him. Or the way he was apparently oblivious to the puppy dog eyes.

They'd left me alone in this room for over an hour. I knew they watched me, probably looking for telltale signs of stress or guilt or whatever silly little human mind games they thought they were playing. I let them have their games if it'd help me get to the bottom of who was stealing souls.

Finally, Jared returned. He sat opposite me and simply looked at me. I looked back. He really did have the most delicious brown eyes, like a swirling mixture of melted chocolate with a gleam of gold. He looked tired, his hair disheveled where he'd run his fingers through it.

"I have a question for you, Detective."

He sat back in surprise.

"What?"

"What brought *you* to the cemetery tonight?"

"The friends of the girl who died called the police. Someone attacked them at the cemetery."

"Attacked them? Did they say what?"

"Don't you mean who?"

"Humans can't steal souls, Detective. What you've got here is a soul stealer. My question is, how did he get to this dimension?"

"I can't believe what I'm hearing."

"I think you do, Detective. You've got yourself one supernatural problem on your hands, and I'm betting this isn't your first brush with the paranormal. What were the girls doing at the cemetery?"

"What impressionable teenage girls do on Halloween. Having a séance. They took an Ouija board out there and were trying to call the spirit of Ruby Bland, a girl who'd died about a hundred years ago and is said to haunt the area."

"It's Halloween? Cool. I love All Hallows' Eve. Are we having a party?"

"What?"

"You're right. No time for that now. How many

girls were at the séance?" I couldn't afford to get distracted. Get in, get the job done, get out.

"Three. Including our victim," he answered automatically.

"Where are the other two?"

"I sent them home with their families. They were distraught. They're coming to the station tomorrow to give statements."

"It's risky."

"What's risky?"

"Well, I'm putting two and two together here and hope I'm getting four. I can't confirm without talking to the girls, *but* I'd say they summoned our soul stealer from a pocket dimension. Not easy to do, but considering it's Halloween, the veil is thin, they just might have fluked it. So they call him forth, and he steps through. Immediately he needs sustenance to survive on this plane. Victim one. That'll hold him for a while. But if he wants to stay here permanently, he has to consume the souls of all who called him."

"All three girls."

"Exactly!" I smiled my approval that he was following along.

"You're telling me the two surviving girls are at risk?"

"Yes." I nodded.

"How can I believe anything you've just told me? It sounds like some far-fetched fairy tale. You were at the scene. Your hands were on the body. How do I know you didn't kill her?"

"I'm not a reaper, Detective. I'm Lucifer. I make sure you're punished for the sins you commit on Earth. I don't take souls—but I can mark them, so they're tagged for Hell."

"Tagged for Hell? What does that even mean?"

"You're not as disbelieving as you make out, Detective. You're a smart guy; work it out. We're wasting time. Our next step should be interviewing those girls and finding out exactly what it is that they saw tonight."

"What you mean is *I* should be interviewing the girls," he corrected me.

I shrugged. One way or another, I'd be talking to those girls.

The door opened, and Detective Nicole James walked in, back straight, hostility rolling off her. Okay, that was unprovoked, but I get it—people respond to me in different ways. This was obviously hers. Hate at first sight.

"I've heard enough of this bullshit." She eyed me

up and down like I was dog shit on her shoe. "Jared, she needs a mental health assessment."

Jared rose from his chair and frowned at her. "Hang on a second, Nic. I'm not done here. Don't be jumping to conclusions." His voice was low, as if he didn't want me to hear, which was impossible since I was seated two feet away. I bit back a laugh.

"No, Jared." She almost, almost, stamped her foot. My lips twitched, and I looked away in case my laughter accidentally escaped.

"She's a person of interest in a homicide. She has no ID, and the story she's been telling indicates that she requires a mental health assessment. I'm holding her."

"Pft. Nothing can hold me, Detective," I piped up with a smirk.

"You're going to have to drop that whole '*I'm Lucifer from Hell*' act," she growled.

"Ah, Detective, your mind is closed. If you would just let yourself, for one second, believe. How the world would open up for you." With a shake of my wrists, the cuffs fell open onto the tabletop. Her mouth dropped open. Even Jared looked surprised.

"How did you do that?" they asked in unison.

"One of my little Lucifer tricks, you know, being an angel and all."

"Quit the bullshit!" Nicole shouted, her face flushing red.

"Calm down, Nic," Jared warned. Clasping a hand around her wrist, he dragged her out of the room, the door banging closed behind them.

"Okaaaay." I arched a perfectly manicured brow and watched the door. Minutes later, he was back. Alone.

"Tell me about tonight. Why were you at the cemetery?"

"I already told you. I was in Hell, doing hellish things, when *beep, beep, beep*, off goes the alarm that someone is up to something nefarious here on Earth. That alarm only goes off when it's B-A-D. World-changing, life-ending bad. So I popped up to see what the fuss is about and found the girl. She was already dead when I got there."

"Did you touch anything?"

"I checked the girl's pulse. She was already dead."

"What about a weapon? Did you see anything that could have been used to kill her?"

"I didn't see anything like that. But then I wasn't looking for it. I was more interested in examining the damage done to her soul."

"We're back to her soul?" He shook his head, but I knew he didn't totally disbelieve my story.

"It was torn from her body, Detective. Ripped away with great violence. There was a lot of damage."

"You're telling me she died because her soul was stolen? And that...what? Brought on a cardiac arrest?"

"You won't find any physical injuries if that's what you're getting at. I'm talking about what your eyes couldn't see. *That* is what's called me to Earth. A soul stealer has found its way into your dimension. It feeds on souls, destroying them, rendering that soul incapable of ascending to Heaven or Hell."

"So this '*soul stealer*' killed her and then stole her soul?" Disbelief clouded his voice.

"He didn't kill her. The violence of having her soul ripped from her caused her to die. It was that act that caused her death. He didn't kill her first, then steal her soul."

"A soul stealer. Jesus, I can't believe I'm saying shit like this," he mumbled, running a weary hand over his face.

"Either way, you have a bad guy to catch,

Detective." Smiling brightly, I rose to my feet, dusting imaginary dust off the back of my black leather pants. I watched as the detective's eyes ran up my body. I knew I looked good. *Come on now, I'm an archangel crafted by God's own hands; I'm stunning.* Everyone thought so. Men and women alike. My hair was jet black and swung to my waist in effortless waves. My skin was smooth as silk and tinted the perfect shade of peach. My body had curves in all the right places. But it was my eyes everyone loved the most. They were the color of sapphires, a dazzling blue. You could drown in them. I wasn't conceited. Just stating a fact. I was an archangel, and my beauty was beyond compare.

Unfortunately, it was the same story for my idiot brothers, Michael and Gabriel. All made by God's hand as archangels. We didn't look the same, but whereas I was stunningly beautiful, they were devastatingly handsome. And I might add, conceited assholes.

I digress. We had a killer to catch, and the key to finding the soul stealer was finding the humans who mistakenly thought it was a good idea to summon one in the first place.

"Shall we go talk to the girls, Detective?" I suggested, already moving toward the door. His hand wrapped around my upper arm in a tight grip, halting my progress.

"Oh no, you don't. It's three-thirty in the morning. The girls are traumatized but hopefully asleep by now. You'll be spending the night in the cells, and tomorrow *I* will interview the girls."

"You really do like your restraints, don't you?" I purred, winking at him as I allowed him to lead me through the station to the cells at the rear of the building. He opened the door of one and ushered me inside. No point in riling him by resisting, I sauntered inside, turning to watch as he locked the door behind me.

"Someone will be by to check on you in the morning. I suggest you spend some time thinking about telling the truth."

I couldn't stop the snort of laughter that followed. "I speak nothing but the truth, Detective. You choose not to believe me."

"Enough already," I heard him mutter beneath his breath, then his footsteps receding, a door closing, a lock turning.

"Ahhhh, humans, how I've missed you. I forgot how funny you can be." I extended my wings with a smile, dematerializing from the cell and appearing at the cemetery less than a second later.

THREE

In the predawn darkness, I could see the restless spirits roaming among the headstones, trekking the path where the now-demolished church-cum-rectory used to stand, disappearing then reappearing to do it all over again.

Initially, they ignored my presence, but they began to feel my energy and were drawn to it. Soon I had a dozen spirits following me across the cemetery to the trees in the corner.

"Which one of you is Ruby Bland?" I asked them.

"I am." A frizzy-haired young woman stepped forward, her grey hospital gown stained with blood.

"Did you see the girls here tonight? The ones trying to communicate with you?"

"I did." Ruby nodded, moving closer, her bare feet making no sound on the ground.

"Did you hurt them?" I didn't think she had, but I had to ask, just to be sure.

"It wasn't I." She shook her head.

"But you saw what happened?"

"I did."

"Tell me."

"He appeared, as if by magic, right in front of the blonde one. He wore a black cloak that covered him from head to toe. He grabbed the blonde's head and kissed her hard, so hard he sucked the very life out of her. As he drew back, you could see it floating like a mist between their mouths. Is he the Grim Reaper?"

"No. No, he's not. He's something much worse. A soul stealer. He feeds on the living."

"When is the reaper coming for me?" she asked, her voice forlorn.

"Has he not been, and you denied him?" I did find it odd that there were so many spirits here.

"No. I wanted to pass. I was ready to go. I want to go now. Can you take me?"

"I'm sorry, Ruby, your soul can't pass through me. I'm not a reaper. But I can send one your way."

"That would be wonderful. I'm bored here."

"I bet. Do you want to tell me how you died?" I offered, knowing Ruby hadn't spoken with anyone in years.

"I had bad pains in my stomach. They took me to the hospital, I was there for days, and then they did an operation to fix me, but they couldn't stop the bleeding. I died." She indicated the blood on her gown. "I hear the stories of what people think happened to me, how they think Father Martin killed me, that I had a baby. I didn't have a baby, and he didn't kill me. But he used to hurt me. He hurt all the girls. Can I go now?" She looked miserable and tired. And who could blame her, left behind on this plane to wander a creepy old cemetery for over a hundred years?

"Sure." I smiled at her before briefly closing my eyes and summoning a reaper. When I opened them again, a man in ripped blue jeans and a white T-shirt stood before us, his blonde hair teased artfully, his lips curled up in a grin.

"You rang?" He did a slight bow to me.

"I've got a customer for you. In fact..." Glancing around the graveyard, I saw several ghosts turn our way as if sensing the reaper's presence and knowing this was their chance to move on. "I think you've got a few misplaced souls here."

"Step right up, folks!" the Reaper joked, spreading his arms wide. "Sorry for the wait."

Ruby shuffled closer, unsure. The reaper turned to her, his soft smile gentle.

"Are you ready, beautiful?" he asked. She nodded. "Then take my hand." He glanced my way. "Is she one of yours?"

"No. I think she's suffered enough. This one is Heaven-bound."

"Gotcha." With a wink, he clasped Ruby's hand in his. She gasped, her eyes grew huge, and a broad smile spread across her face. Then she was gone.

The reaper dusted his hands on his jeans and looked at the dozen ghosts who were now crowding around us in a circle.

"Anyone else?" The ghosts moved forward en masse, all eager to leave this world. I stepped back out of the way and let the reaper do his thing. Not all the ghosts crossed. Some were stuck, probably always would be, their unfinished business destined to remain incomplete, their minds destroyed by the weight of their loss.

"Care to tell me why you hadn't come to help these guys out before now?" I asked.

The reaper shrugged. "Super busy these days. There are only six of us, and we never get a moment's respite, what with all the war and terrorism happening. Sadly a lot of souls get left behind. We need more resources to do a sweep of the spirit world. I can feel there is a Hell of a lot more still waiting in this town alone."

"Have you put in a request to God? Surely he'd be amicable to assisting the reapers?"

"We've put in several requests. Can't get past the gatekeepers."

"The gatekeepers?"

"Michael and Gabriel. They keep a tight rein on who gets access to God. So far as I know, it's only them. No one has seen him in eons. All requests come back denied." He glanced off in the distance for a moment before dragging his gaze back to mine. "Gotta go. There's been a bombing in Paris." Before I had a chance to tell him about our soul stealer problem, he'd vanished.

I walked amongst the headstones, tried talking a time or two with the ghosts that remained, but it was as if they were oblivious to my presence, their eyes unseeing, focused on things I couldn't see, trapped in a never-ending cycle of...whatever it was that held them here. It was sad.

I wondered why God wasn't helping them. Surely this wasn't what he'd intended, that people would become trapped, unable to move on. As far as I knew, the plan had been that their soul moved to Heaven or Hell when a person died. That's it. Those were your choices. Not this limbo of being trapped in a physical realm. And why wasn't he sending help for the reapers? Not to mention all this war that the reaper had mentioned. He was right: the amount of violence across the globe had escalated. It needed to be stopped. Why didn't God visit, guide his creations back onto the right path? Or was he done with them, letting them slowly drive themselves into extinction? It puzzled me, and I made a mental note to take the time to visit him, maybe invite him to Hell, show him firsthand what I'd achieved.

I sank down onto a bench at the side of the cemetery and watched as pink and orange streaks of dawn broke across the sky, pondering what could possibly be happening in Heaven that kept God away. I stayed a long time after the sun rose, enjoying the warmth of it on my skin, but eventually, I roused myself. *Better return to the police station, I suppose.* I was just getting ready to leave when I felt it, the ripple in time as an angel appeared behind me.

I spun, expecting to see Michael or Gabriel and berate them for taking so long to get here. Instead, it was Dacian, my best friend who'd trained with me in the dawn of time. We'd spent hours together talking and playing. We'd been the four amigos, Dacian, Michael, Gabriel, and me. Although Dacian wasn't an archangel, God had taken a shine to him and welcomed him into the fold.

"Dacian!" I launched myself into his arms, wrapping him tight in an embrace. "It's so good to see you. It's been ages. How are you? And where are Michael and Gabriel? They should be here to help."

Dacian stood stiffly in my embrace, arms by his sides. I pulled back, frowning. What was wrong with him?

"Dacian? What's wrong?" He jerked out of my arms and took a step back, his dark brows pulled together in a frown. God, he looked good, just as hot as I remembered, his dark hair tousled like he'd just rolled out of bed, a light dusting of stubble across his jaw, his blue eyes sparkling. Correction. His blue eyes weren't so much sparkling as glowering. What the Hell?

"How do you know my name?" he demanded.

"What do you mean 'how do I know your name'? We used to hang out together. In Heaven. Don't you remember?"

"We"—he indicated the two of us—"did no such

thing."

"Sure we did. You, me, Michael and Gabriel. We used to play in the Garden of Eden, hang out with Adam and Eve. You taught me how to spar." He was shaking his head.

"No. You were not there. It was me, Michael and Gabriel who did these things. You must have been spying on them, even then."

"What? Spying? Don't be ridiculous. I'm an archangel, along with my brothers."

"You lie. Gabriel and Michael are the only archangels. You are Lucifer, fallen angel, creator of evil, and ruler of Hell."

My eyes sparked flames for an instant. Fallen angel, my ass. It was bad enough having the humans think me an evil demon, but my own kind? Excuse the cliché, but what the Hell was going on?

"I'm here to deliver a message." His voice was as cold as ice, not the warm, friendly, funny Dacian that I remembered so fondly.

"Which is?" I sighed, planning a trip to Heaven to bang my brother's heads together...just what were they doing up there?

"Return to Hell. Immediately. You have no place on Earth."

"No can do, my friend." I spun on my heel and

began walking toward the cemetery gate. "In case my brothers haven't noticed, there's a soul stealer on the loose."

"An evil creature of your own creation that you intentionally brought to this plane."

"Are you friggin serious?" I glanced over my shoulder at him following behind me. "Did you have a blow to the head?"

"You are ordered to return to the underworld," he grated, anger coloring his words.

"I take orders from no one. Least of all you and my pathetic brothers." His hand clamping down hard on my shoulder stopped me in my tracks. He spun me around to face him, his wings extended behind him, magnificent and splendid in their blazing white. Only he held them in an attack pose. Oh really? He wanted to rumble? *Bring it on!* I extend my own wings, six-foot either side, my once-white feathers now black with flames dancing across the surface. You get that after millennia in Hell.

"What happened to your wings?" His frown was back, but at least the sight of my wings had thrown him off his intention of fighting with me.

"They evolved. Working in Hell with flames, fire, and soot, it's impossible to keep anything clean. Black is the new white."

"And the flames?"

"I'm the Devil." I shrugged. My flames only burnt if I wished them to, which was never. But they were intimidating and made a good threat. Some of the truly evil souls were hard to crack, and it took displays of my strength and power to break them. But to repent for your sins, you had to be broken down so that you could be rebuilt.

"Are you going to return to Hell?"

"Nope."

He launched at me, but I danced out of the way. I was quicker, faster, more experienced than he'd ever been. True, he'd taught me how to spar. Once. And then the student had become the teacher. It made my heart ache to think he didn't remember any of it, of our time together, our friendship. And it puzzled me why. Angels didn't suffer memory loss. Something had happened to him, and I needed to find out what.

My own pondering was my downfall. While I was distracted, he tackled me to the ground, spear diving me. His arms wrapped around my waist, and we slid along the ground, my wings dragging in the gravel, stinging. He brought one white wing around in front to press against my throat while he straddled me. A wave of sadness filled me, not that we were fighting or that I was worried he would hurt me, but that the Dacian I knew and loved had changed so much. Of all the things, that was what hurt.

"Your eyes," he muttered, frowning.

"What about them?" I pouted.

"They look...sad."

"I am sad." I agreed with his assessment.

"Because I beat you?" he gloated.

"Pft. You haven't beaten me, Angel. I'm sad that you don't remember me. Our past."

He stiffened. "Your lies again."

"No. Not lies, Dacian. How would I know your name if we hadn't met before?"

"Spies."

"I'm far too busy running my own plane to worry about yours, sweetheart. Why would I bother spying on you or my brothers?"

He seemed at a loss, thinking about what I said.

"Let me try something," I asked.

"What?" He eyed me suspiciously.

"Trust me."

"You can't be trusted."

"Just let me try this one thing. I promise I won't hurt you or try and get away."

"What are you going to do?"

"Move your wing from my throat."

He looked down at me for several moments before slowly removing his wing. I reached up and gently laid my hands on his cheeks and pulled his head toward me. Rising up to meet him, I settled my lips softly against his and projected all of my memories of us to him. The fun we'd had, the laughter, games, and over time—attraction. The day he'd stolen a kiss. Our mutual delight. I stopped the memories there, didn't share with him the chaos over what had happened in the Garden of Eden, the betrayal of my brothers, my heartache at leaving him. Slowly I released him from my hold and lay back on the ground watching as he closed his eyes for a moment.

"You planted those visions. They aren't memories, just your twisted fantasies."

"You're trying my patience, Dacian," I growled, flipping him off me and rising to my feet. This time it was my wing pressed against his throat, the flames dancing across his skin, yet not burning.

"Tell my brothers this. I will not be returning to Hell until the soul stealer is dealt with. End of story. If you're not here to assist, don't bother coming back."

FOUR

With a flap of my wings, I materialized in front of the police station. I strolled inside, smiling at the officer behind the front counter, who reacted by drawing a gun and pointing it at me.

"Freeze!" she yelled, then over her shoulder, "She's here. Out front. Backup!" The foyer was suddenly a bustle of activity. Another office flung open a side door and ran toward me, spun me into the wall, and clapped handcuffs around my wrists. I bit back a smile, letting them think they had the upper hand, that they had me under control. Jared appeared, frowning at me.

"How did you get out?" he demanded.

"I flew out," I told him.

"Flew out?"

"With my wings?" I wiggled one shoulder at him.

"If you could fly, why would you come back?"

"Because we have unfinished business, Detective. There's a soul stealer on the loose. This isn't the time for bailing."

He sighed and ran a hand around the back of his neck.

"Put her in interview room two."

The officer who'd cuffed me grabbed me by the upper arm and dragged me through the station to a door with the number two stenciled on it. Pushing me inside, he closed the door with a terse, "Stay put."

I slipped the cuffs off and laid them on the table before sliding onto the rather uncomfortable chair they'd provided. It was warm in the room, my leather pants, bustier, and coat soon sticking to my skin. In the blink of an eye, I switched outfits into a figure-hugging Alexander McQueen red dress that had cut-out sides and stopped several inches above my knees. Louis Vuitton heels in the exact same shade as my dress encased my feet.

Energy thrummed through the building, making the hairs on my arms stand on end. It could only mean one thing. The girls were here. And if I could feel them, well, I had to assume the soul stealer could as well. I'd have to remedy that, pronto. While it was tempting to leave the station and begin the search for the items I'd need for a couple of warding talismans, I didn't want to give the detective a brain aneurysm, so for the moment, I sat tight. While I waited, I listened to the girls giving their statements, their descriptions of last night's events matching what Ruby had already told me.

A couple of hours had passed when I felt the girls' energy shift and move. Then I could hear the detective explaining that he wanted them to see me and identify me as the person they'd seen at the cemetery. I plastered a bored look on my face and sat staring at the wall, knowing they were observing me through the two-way mirror. I turned and looked their way, studying them as they studied me, the mirror useless against me. They were pretty. One had short dark hair cut in a bob, her skin a tanned mocha. She was tall and slim, her dark eyes reflecting her pain, her cheeks tear-streaked. The girl next to her was a similar height and build. Her skin was pale, her brown hair hung long and straight almost to her waist. She trembled ever so slightly.

"Brianna? Do you recognize her?" The detective addressed the short-haired girl. Brianna. I filed her name away.

"No. It definitely wasn't her. It was a man, I'm sure of it. Tall and very broad. Huge."

"Sarah? What about you?"

"It wasn't her. We've already told you."

"Have you seen this woman before?"

"Never. She wasn't at the cemetery. Not when we were there." Sarah swiped a tear from her cheek, turning to the older woman standing behind them. "Can we go home now, Mom?"

"Sure, honey, if it's okay with the detective."

"Yes, you can go. Call me if you remember anything else. No matter how small or incidental a detail might be, it can all help."

"Sure," Sarah all but whispered, then wrapped her arms around Brianna, hugging her tight.

"Come on, girls. I'll drop you home to your gran, Brianna." Sarah's mother ushered them away.

The door opened, and the detective stood frowning at me.

"What happened to your clothes?" he demanded. His voice may have been curt, but the look on his face as his eyes traveled the length of my body was one of appreciation.

I shrugged. "It was getting hot in here. I changed."

"How? You didn't have anything with you when we brought you in."

I crossed the room and patted his cheek. "Don't stress, Detective, my clothing is the least of your worries. So I take it I'm free to go? Brianna and Sarah confirmed I wasn't the one who hurt their friend."

"How did you know that? This room is virtually soundproof."

"Not to these angel ears." I smiled again, then shuffled past him in the open doorway.

"As much as I'd love to hang around and chat, Detective, those girls are still in danger. I need to rustle up a couple of talismans to protect them." I could feel his eyes boring into my back as I walked away.

Outside it was a beautiful day, the chill of the night forgotten with the rising of the sun. Summer wasn't far away. I stood for a moment to get my bearings. The police station stood opposite the town hall, in between was the town square, as if the two buildings were standing sentinel over the picturesque marquee in the middle of the square. All around were quaint shops, cafes, hair salons. Shadow Falls was a very picturesque town. I liked it.

I crossed the road to the town square. Keeping my eyes peeled, I wandered along, letting the warmth of the sun sink into my skin. It wasn't until I was here on Earth, breathing in the air, feeling the breeze in my hair and the warmth of the sun, that I realized how much I'd missed it. Hell was a whole lot warmer, but we didn't have the sun. Our skies were a perpetual swirl of orange, red, and pink clouds, mystically lit. We didn't have seasons; it was constant.

Finally, I saw what I was looking for. The Black Hat. Not literally a black hat, but a new age shop with purple signage of an eighteenth-century woman in a long dress complete with bustle, parasol, and black hat. As I pushed open the door, the bell above it jangled, announcing my presence.

From the back of the shop, a voice rang out. "Be with you in a minute."

"Take your time, Levi," I called back. Levi Forrester, clairvoyant, twenty-eight human years, hundreds as an old soul. A man I was very interested in meeting. A man who had me curious. A man who'd sent me a vision, connecting with me from a different realm.

He poked his head around a shelf to eyeball me, then stepped forward. His brown hair was cut short in the back, longer in front, and brushed up into some sort of messy quiff. His eyes were the same as when I'd seen them on the monitor, a gorgeous shade of hazel mixed with gold, and he still sported the light beard that I had a sudden desire to run my fingers over. Wearing jeans and a T-shirt, well-worn Converse on his feet, he was the exact opposite of Detective Jared Morrison, who, while very pleasant to look at in his crisp suit, was nothing compared to what the sight of Levi Forrester did to my insides. My attraction to him was immediate, and I wondered if it was due to his clairvoyant abilities, the otherworldly nature of it, for I could feel it on him, and it made me want to purr.

"How do you know my name?" he asked, stepping forward, his eyes running over me, the gold in them smoldering, the flash of desire unguarded. My heart leaped in my chest, and I placed a hand over it. The unbidden reaction surprised me.

"I know most things." I shrugged. "I'm Lucifer. Call me Lucy."

"You're...you're...a woman." He blew out a surprised breath.

"Correct." I waited patiently for him to gather his thoughts. I knew everyone thought Lucifer was a male, thrown out of Heaven to the depths of Hell for his sins. Truth be told, that was a load of bullshit made up by my brothers. Unfortunately, that old wives' tale stuck.

You want to know the true story? The truth was after God created Heaven and Earth and gave his precious little humans free will, well, certain individuals chose the evil path. So when their time on Earth was up, they ended up in Heaven with all the angelic souls, wreaking havoc. God realized his mistake and subsequently created Hell, where souls could be punished for their misdeeds. It also ensured that those in Heaven behaved themselves. And he asked me to run it. I was not thrown out of Heaven. I was promoted.

"Is God a woman?" Levi asked.

"No." I shook my head.

"There goes that theory," he cursed, wiping his palms on his thighs.

"It would've been nice, I agree."

"So you are Lucifer. Lucy. The fallen angel."

It was my time to sigh and shake my head. "Not fallen. I'm still an archangel. I rule Hell. I ensure you are punished for your sins before you can ascend to Heaven. It is an honor, not a banishment."

"Right!" His smile was dazzling. "That makes perfect sense."

I smiled in return, pleased he'd believed me. Though why it mattered whether a human believed me or not, I couldn't say. Who was I kidding? Of course, it mattered what Levi thought of me. I was drawn to him like a magnet. That not only intrigued me, but it also brought out my feminine sensibilities. I *wanted* him to like me.

"The detectives have a bigger problem believing me."

"Who? Jared and Nic?" At my nod, he rushed on. "Jared's okay. Sometimes he just needs a little time to get his head around things, but he's fairly open. I've worked with him a time or two. As for Nic? She's tighter than a duck's ass. She's a by-the-book, do-not-deviate, no-shades-of-gray type gal."

"Yeah, I got that." I laughed.

"So..." He paused and looked me up and down, and I felt the heat radiate from his gaze, "Not to be rude or anything, but what are you doing here? In my shop?" he clarified.

"You sent me a message, Levi."

"I did?" I wasn't surprised by his surprise. He had no idea how strong or deep his powers were.

"You saw the death of the girl. Emily Barlow. You projected it to me."

He wiped a hand around the back of his neck

and blew out a breath. "That was intense! I was doing a reading for a client, and BOOM, it hit me. I could sense something, I don't know what, then I saw her body fall. She was dead before she hit the ground."

"Did you see the soul stealer?"

"I saw a dark, shadowy figure wearing a long black cloak with a hood obscuring his face. He grabbed the girl by the neck and *kissed* her. And she dropped down dead."

I nodded. That matched what Ruby Bland had said.

"He's a soul stealer? For real?" Levi asked.

"Yes. From a pocket dimension. They unwittingly summoned him with a séance out at the cemetery."

"Oh man, these kids messing about in stuff they don't understand. Haven't they watched enough horror movies to know that contacting the dead can have some serious negative juju?" He ran his hands through his hair in apparent frustration. I couldn't disagree with him. Nor could I take my eyes off him. "Anyway, to get back to your question. I felt him like a tug on my magic, so I tuned in to see if I could channel what was going on. That's when I saw what happened. Then it ended, but suddenly there was a flash of radiant energy. Nearly knocked me out, but I couldn't see what it was."

"Probably me arriving," I told him.

"That explains it." He nodded. "I've felt you ever since. You're like an electrical hum."

"I can feel you too, which is one of the reasons why I'm here."

"Oh?" I almost told him of the delicious feelings he was arousing in me but swallowed them down. My libido may be raging, but lives were at stake, I scolded myself. "We need to make a couple of talismans to protect the remaining girls. He'll come back for them. He needs to take their souls to bind himself to this plane permanently. We can't allow that to happen. The only way to protect them is to hide them from him."

Levi shifted his weight from one foot to the other. "Just tell me what you need."

The talismans were deceptively simple to make. One for each bracelet, a leather cord, and a blue crystal, which I subsequently infused with my power. When they were complete, I held them up in my hand.

"Perfect! Now to get them to the girls."

"I can take you. I know where Sarah lives, and Brianna is probably with her."

I waited while Levi locked up his shop, then followed him outside. A dented old Volkswagen van was parked out the back, and I sank into the passenger seat, admiring the old car.

"Picked it up for five hundred bucks—can you believe it?" he told me, turning the key in the ignition. The engine fired to life, settling into a soft rumble.

"I'm going to do it up one day, total engine rebuild, bodywork, paint, and upholstery job. It'll cost a bit, but it'll be worth it." Levi lovingly patted a hand on the dashboard.

I failed to see why a human would form a bond with a vehicle, but Levi and his van clearly had one, so who was I to tarnish it? I smiled and settled back, listening to his chatter as we drove through the streets before pulling up ten minutes later in front of a typical suburban home. Something about being near Levi was soothing to me, and again I wondered about the connection I had with him. I looked at him as we climbed out of the van, his loose-limbed walk, the way the breeze ruffled his hair. When he caught me looking, he raised a brow, and his lip curled up in a grin, and I wanted to touch him. Reach out my hand and run my fingers across those lips. Press my own lips against his and see what he tasted like.

These thoughts, as delicious as they were, were also foreign to me. Why did I feel so obsessed with him? He was virtually a stranger. And a human at that. While I'd had lovers in the past, they'd never drawn out such feelings in me, and to say it was unsettling was an understatement. Snapping my attention away from him, I strode to the front door, feeling him behind me as we waited for the doorbell to be answered.

"Yes?" The woman I'd seen at the police station, Sarah Moore's mother, opened the door and looked at us.

"Mrs. Moore, I was hoping to speak with Sarah, please. And Brianna if she's here." I smiled my most non-threatening smile.

"The girls aren't seeing anyone at the moment." She started to close the door. I reached out and grabbed it.

"Please, Mrs. Moore. I'll only be a minute. It's really important." I pushed just a little bit of compulsion into my voice. Using too much could send her into a comatose state, and I didn't want that.

She looked at us both again, her eyes darting

between us before she let out a sigh. Letting go of the door, she ushered us inside. "Upstairs. First door on the left."

The girls were both lying on the bed when we walked in, notebooks spread out in front of them with what looked like fashion designs sketched on the pages.

"Hi, Sarah. Hi, Brianna. Sorry to intrude. I'm Lucy, and you probably already know Levi."

"We know you. You were at the police station. Detective James said you'd killed Emily." Sarah sat up, tossing her long dark hair over her shoulder.

"Sarah," Brianna warned, "she didn't say that at all. She insinuated it, which is entirely different."

"I didn't hurt your friend," I assured them.

"We know that." Brianna smiled weakly.

"A séance, eh?" I moved further into the room, looking around at the pictures on the wall.

"Girls, haven't I warned you before about messing with that stuff?" Levi scolded, sitting down on the end of the bed and snatching the notebook away from Sarah to begin flicking through the pages.

"Hey, these are good." Surprise colored his voice.

"We're designing our Halloween costumes."

"Wasn't Halloween last night?" I was confused.

"Well yeah, technically, but since it's a weeknight, the school is holding a Halloween party this weekend."

"Sounds like fun." I loved a good party myself, but... "Sorry, girls, but this one is a no-go."

"No go? What?" Brianna frowned.

"Not to be alarmist—well, actually, I'm probably going to have to take that back because what I'm about to tell you is, well, alarming."

"What!?" the girls practically shouted. I held up a hand to hush them.

"Your friend, Emily, was killed by a soul stealer. You opened a portal to another dimension during your séance, and he got through."

"Are you for real?" Sarah's voice was somewhere between sarcasm and fear.

"I'm very much for real. The reason I'm here is to give you these." I pulled out the talisman bracelets. "These will hide you from the soul stealer. Wear them. At all times. They're never to come off, not until I tell you."

"Hide us? Why? Are we in danger?" Brianna asked, watching as Levi fastened the bracelet around her wrist.

"Yes." I had no choice but to be blunt. There was no sugar-coating this. "If the soul stealer is to stay on earth permanently, he has to consume your souls."

"Consume our souls? As in...kill us?" Brianna whispered.

"Correct. Naturally, I'm not going to let that happen. I'm going to send his sorry ass back to his own dimension, *but* in the meantime, you need protection, and this is it." I indicated their bracelets.

"How can a piece of jewelry protect us?" Sarah's tone was disbelieving.

"Because I have placed a concealment charm on it. During the séance, the soul stealer was able to get a lock on your individual essences, meaning he can find you, anytime, anywhere. There is no hiding. But as long as you're wearing the talisman, you are, in fact, hidden. Safe. He cannot find you."

"We'll wear them, I promise." Brianna touched her bracelet. "You did it up properly, didn't you?" she asked Levi. "It won't come undone, fall off?"

"It's secure." Levi nodded, resting his hand on Brianna's shoulder to reassure her. I watched Sarah, who was fiddling with her bracelet. I was worried about her. Even though she'd witnessed her friend's death, I sensed she didn't honestly believe any of this.

"Sarah?" I pushed a little compulsion her way. "You'll leave the bracelet on, right?"

"Yes."

Satisfied the compulsion had worked, I continued, "While the soul stealer can't track you, if he sees you—anywhere—and recognizes you? The bracelets won't help you. They can't protect you from an attack—they can only keep you hidden. As long as you're sensible. Which means no parties."

"But—" Sarah began, but Brianna spoke over her.

"We won't go. I'd rather miss a party and stay alive." She glared at Sarah, who shut her mouth against any more protests.

"Give me your phones," Levi demanded, hand out. Brianna held hers out, and Levi took it, quickly typing something in before handing it back. He did the same with Sarah's.

"That's my number. If anything happens. Anything. Call me."

"The police said to call them," Sarah grumbled.

"Call me first. Believe me, the two of us are going to be of more help than the police if the soul stealer catches up with you."

CHAPTER

FIVE

By the time we returned to Levi's shop, the sun was dipping on the horizon, and the warmth of the day had seeped away. I changed from my dress into blue jeans, boots, and a T-shirt with the word *Devil* emblazoned across the front.

"Neat trick." Levi's eyes ran along my long legs encased in denim, and I felt the heat of his gaze as if he'd touched me.

"I can do almost anything. I'm an archangel." My stomach suddenly made a loud gurgling noise, and I placed a hand over it. "What was that?" My body had never made such a sound before.

Levi laughed. "That was your stomach rumbling. You're hungry. You need food."

"Oh!"

"Don't you eat food in Hell?"

"Well, yes, but my body has never demanded it before."

"Your body must be adjusting to being here then because we need to refuel several times a day." Levi eyed me up and down, and I felt the searing heat of his gaze as it traced a path from the top of my head to my toes and back again. A ripple of desire speared through me, and I was intrigued again at the reaction that I had, not to all humans, but this one in particular.

"What a design flaw," I muttered. "I'm surprised Father didn't rectify that."

"Come on, let's get you fed. Have you eaten at all today?"

I shook my head.

"No wonder you're hungry. You've missed breakfast and lunch. Come on, we'll get you an early dinner." Levi flipped the sign on his shop door to closed again, muttering under his breath that today was a write-off anyway. We walked down the sidewalk side by side, coming to a stop in front of a café. The sign on the window said *Falls Coffee*.

Following Levi inside, I slid into a booth opposite him. At the counter stood the two

Detectives, Jared and Nic, who appeared to be ordering coffee. I watched the waitress serve them and frowned. She didn't like them. Or she didn't like Nic, which wasn't surprising. The female detective was prickly. It was no wonder she alienated many of the townsfolk. As if sensing me watching her, the waitress looked up, her eyes meeting mine. With a dramatic sigh at the inconvenience of having to wait on our table, she grabbed her order pad, told the detectives she'd be back in a moment, and made her way toward where Levi and I were seated.

Jared glanced over his shoulder, then turned fully when he recognized me. I winked at him and smiled at the light blush of color that rose in his face. He was easy to tease.

"You ready to order?" The waitress asked, pen poised. I glanced at her name tag, then leaned forward.

"I sure am, Sophie. Let me begin by saying I know what you do, and if you don't cut it out, I've got a special spot reserved for you. In Hell."

Her eyes shot to mine, and I allowed the flames of Hell to dance in my gaze. I knew she saw because I could see it reflected back in her own eyes. She swallowed, stuttering, "Wh...what do you mean?"

"Fine, you want me to spell it out? I will because

I don't want any misunderstandings between us. I know you spit in the food of the people who didn't leave you a tip the last time they were here. That's not a very nice thing for you to be doing now, Sophie, is it?"

"I guess not," she whispered, face pale.

"It stops now." I lightly touched the back of her hand, and she hurriedly snatched it away, dissipating the black mist that had gathered.

"What did you just do?" she accused.

"Marked you. Any more misdemeanors on your behalf, and when your time is up, you'll be coming to visit me. In Hell. Did I mention I'm Lucifer?" Again I let the fires of Hell glow through my eyes. Her crime wasn't huge, but it wasn't nice either, and small things, left unchecked, can escalate into big things. If I could save her soul here and now, all the better.

"I understand. I'm sorry," she whispered, hands shaking.

I blinked, masking the burning in my gaze, and smiled at her. "I'm ready to order now. How about you, Levi?"

Levi cleared his throat. "Errr, yeah. Sure."

After we placed our orders and the waitress hurried off, I let my gaze linger on Jared, who had watched my interaction with the waitress from across the room. I couldn't read his expression, but I thought I caught a hint of understanding, a dawning of comprehension. Either that or he was constipated.

"Can I ask you something?"

I brought my attention back to Levi, who was watching me with raised brows. I nodded. "What was that? With your eyes?"

"Sophie has been doing something that, if left unchecked, could possibly escalate into full-on... sinning...and earn her a place in my home. I let her know that," I explained.

"Can I see?" He sounded genuinely curious, so I figured, why not? Levi was a good man, he wasn't slated for Hell, but that's not to say he hadn't made mistakes. He'd made plenty. But he'd repented and made good what he could. That was what mattered. I let the fires of Hell glow through my eyes, so he got a nice close-up view of what Sophie saw.

"Right," he said, peering into my eyes, leaning closer until I could feel his breath on my face. I blinked, extinguishing the flames, and he straightened abruptly, leaning back against his chair.

"No offense, but that was awful." A look of

disgust flitted across his face, and I tensed at the unexpected barb.

"You don't like my eyes?"

"Not with the flames in them. That's more than creepy." He shuddered, then went on, oblivious to my hurt—though why I should be hurt he didn't like my eyes was another thing I filed away to examine later. "I thought they'd be, like, solid black, like you see on the TV shows. The flames are..."

"They're fucking awesome is what they are." I cut across him, affronted that he'd prefer my eyes be a solid pit of black.

"I've upset you." Realization dawned. He reached across the table and captured my hand, his face sincere. "I didn't mean to insult you. I'm sorry. Sometimes I speak without thinking—I open my mouth, and words fall out. Sorry." The warmth of his hand on mine heated my skin until a tingling began, working its way from my hand, up my arm, across my chest. I dragged in a breath, the scent of him filling my lungs. He was musk and chocolate and whiskey and earth. Deep, dark, and inviting. I wondered if he'd taste the same, ran my tongue across my lips as if I could taste him there.

His hazel eyes darkened, then lowered, watching my mouth. His own lips parted, and my thighs clenched. I hadn't had a lover in a long time, hadn't been interested if the truth be told, but Levi Forrester? He was very interesting indeed. There was something primal about him, the way his eyes trailed over me, burning a fiery path everywhere they touched, and suddenly I was ravenous. Only not for food.

The clatter of a plate being put down in front of me startled me, shattering the fantasy of stripping Levi naked and kissing him until he was growling beneath me. Fanning my hand over my heated cheeks, I shifted my attention away from him, watching Sophie's ramrod-straight back as she stalked away from our table and back to the front counter. The barista had finished the order Jared and Nic were patiently waiting for. Sophie collected the steaming cups and placed them on the counter, carefully pushing the lids on and sliding the cups towards the detectives. "Have a nice day now." She smiled, although it didn't reach her eyes. Nic picked up her coffee and swiveled, in a hurry to be out of the café.

Jared eyed his coffee. He slowly picked it up, looking from it to Sophie and back again several times before turning and looking at me. I arched a brow.

Nic turned back, clearly puzzled why Jared wasn't following her. "Jared? You coming?"

Without taking his eyes off me, he answered, "Yeah." He waited another second before following her out of the café.

Turning my attention to my food, I lifted the burger I'd ordered to my mouth and took a bite. Closing my eyes on a sigh, I chewed and swallowed. The food was delicious. I could see how the humans got addicted to it.

"Tell me about Hell." Levi had almost finished his burger and was squirting sauce over his fries.

"It's beautiful." I smiled, thinking of my home. "Not as big as Earth, but big enough. The sky is a swirling combination of pinks, reds, and oranges. It's unlike anything you've ever seen before."

"I've never imagined Hell as being beautiful." He cocked his head to one side. "Where do you live? As in, do you have...houses? A cave?"

"A cave? Seriously?"

"Sorry. I'm insulting you again. All I know about Hell is that it's all fire and brimstone."

"It's neither of those things." I could see I had some educating to do. "Hell is basically one massive city. There's a large expanse of flat land that drops off a deep cliff. At the bottom of the cliff is the pit—

yes, the fire pit, but that is the only place in Hell you'll find fire. Hell HQ is perched on the edge of the cliff top. It's the tallest building in Hell, and I can see for eternity."

"So all the souls are in the pit?"

"Nope. Only the really bad ones. Not every evil person deserves the pit. But they still deserve punishment, so we have hundreds of cells, all housed in high-rise prisons for want of a better word. Only we don't simply incarcerate. We punish. I punish. It's not about taking your freedom. It's about punishment. So depending on what you've done, I'll craft a punishment unique to each individual who graces my doorstep."

"Such as?"

"Such as being locked in a room with your greatest fear, or make you relive the worst moment of your life, over and over. Or I could take it up a notch, string you up with hooks through your flesh."

Levi shuddered. "That's so gross."

"I never said it was pretty."

"And no one leaves? Ever?"

"Yes, souls can leave. They can ascend to Heaven once their punishment is complete. Some are with me for a short time, some are with me for a lifetime. Time doesn't pass the same way it does here on earth. Ten minutes here is like ten years in Hell. If you're having your bones broken over and over...can you imagine? The pain and torture going on for ten years? Would you have repented by then? I break you down, down to your very last molecule, and rebuild you into a better person. Then, and only then, can you leave."

"I'm sure everyone would be sorry for their sins as soon as they turn up on your doorstep."

"True. Words are meaningless in Hell. I have to feel it. You can scream at me that you've repented, that you're sorry, that you're different, a better person. Until I feel it, your punishment continues."

Levi was silent, mulling over my words, nodding slightly as he took it all in.

Returning my attention to my food, I finished the burger and half of the fries. Then I leaned back, settled my hands over my now full stomach, and smiled. I'd have to remember to keep my body fuelled while I was here.

"You ready? I'll settle up, and then we can get out of here." Levi wiped his mouth on a napkin then pulled the slip of paper Sophie had left on our table toward him. Flipping it over, he examined what was written there, then pulled out his wallet and left a handful of notes with the paper. Noticing me watching him, he raised his eyebrows, then nodded to himself.

"This"—he picked up the piece of paper and waved it at me—"is our bill. For the food." He put the paper down and picked up the dollar bills. "And this is the money I'm leaving to pay for the food." I almost laughed. I knew how it worked, knew what he was doing, but I didn't want to hurt his feelings, so I played along.

"Do you leave a tip?" I was curious. Had Sophie been spitting in Levi's food?

"Of course!" Levi seemed shocked that I'd ask. "So you know about tips? I heard what you said to Sophie but wasn't sure."

I knew pretty much everything that went on in this plane, for I kept an eye on things on my monitors. I'd watched over the years as the humans progressed from the stone age, created fanciful inventions, and technology progressed. I'd watched as the free will Father insisted they have made them do horrible, evil things to each other.

"Never mind." Pushing to my feet, I waited for Levi to slide out of the booth. I cast my eyes over the other diners in the café. It was early, but several people had decided on an early dinner or a late afternoon snack, one of which drew my attention. A young boy, ten years old, sitting with his mother, both enjoying a milkshake.

"Hang on a second," I told Levi, crossing the room to stand next to their table. Levi moved to the door, arms crossed, watching, while the mother and her son both looked at me curiously.

"Yes?" the mother asked. "Can I help you?"

"Lucas here has been a naughty boy," I told her, watching as Lucas's brown eyes rounded in fright. *Yeah, you are so busted, buddy.*

"What? Who are you? How do you know my son?"

"Lucas has been bullying the other kids at school, threatening them, even hurting them, forcing them to give him their lunch."

The woman sucked in a breath. Her eyes, the same color as her son's, swiveled from me to him, and she leaned forward, elbows on the table, and peered at him intently.

"Is this true?"

Lucas swallowed. He was an overweight little boy, and his mother had put him on a diet, concerned not only for his health but his future. Other kids teased the fat kids. Only what she didn't know was he was cheating, stealing food from the other kids. He, in fact, was the bully. And this little mommy-son date with the milkshakes was his special treat for doing so well on his diet.

Lucas looked at me again, and I let the flames dance in my eyes. He quickly looked back to his mom and nodded, his head bowed. "Yes," he mumbled.

"Lucas!" Her outrage was evident in her tone. She turned to me, and I could see it all: how tired she was, how difficult Lucas was at home, how her husband was of little help.

"Lucas, look at me." I crouched by the table, so we were eye to eye and let him see what he needed to see. "The bad behavior has got to stop, my man, understand me?"

He nodded so hard and so fast I feared his head might topple off.

"Good. I hope we don't meet again."

I left the café knowing two souls were saved today. It might not be much, but if I could stop them from turning up on my doorstep, I'd call that a win.

Levi's apartment was above his shop, and it was small. I was pretty sure my shoe closet was bigger than his entire apartment.

"Sorry about the mess." A hint of color dusted his cheeks. It wasn't so much that his home was messy. It was more that he had a lot of stuff and not enough space for it. Books were piled upon each other on almost every surface. An old sofa dominated the living room, more books piled up on one end. Across the room, a tiny kitchen, an old wooden table that had seen better days, and one dining chair. Two doors led off the living area. One was Levi's bedroom, the other the bathroom.

A small four-legged creature rubbed itself around Levi's legs and made a strange noise. I couldn't contain my squeal. Jumping behind Levi, holding his shoulders to keep him between me and the creature, I practically screamed, "What the Hell is that?"

"Mr. Meow. My cat." Levi frowned at me as if I were insane.

"That's not a cat!" I protested. "Cats are fluffy and cute. That...that...thing is not a cat. It has no fur."

Levi reached down and scooped Mr. Meow into his arms, stroking his palm down its back. Mr. Meow purred in response, headbutting Levi's chin. I stepped away, frowning. When had this happened? When had they created cats with no fur? Levi clearly loved this butt ugly creature, and I was struggling to see the appeal.

"I love cats, but I'm allergic," he explained, his face telling me he was affronted that I didn't adore his pet.

"I can fix that," I promised. Stepping forward, I placed my hand on his forehead and pushed some healing energy into him. Any health complaints Levi had were now gone.

"What did you do?" He eyed me suspiciously.

"I cured your allergy. Now let me fix your cat. Geez, the poor thing must be freezing with no fur." I gingerly placed my hand on top of Mr. Meow's head and, before our eyes, the cat grew fur. A gorgeous tortoiseshell coat of black, white, and tan. "That's better."

"What do you think, Mr. Meow?" Levi asked, holding Mr. Meow so they were nose to nose. "Do you like having fur?" Mr. Meow meowed and licked his paw. Laughing, Levi set him on the floor where he wound himself in and out of Levi's legs, purring even louder than before.

"I think he likes it!"

"Of course he does." I plopped down onto the only clear space on the sofa, glad that the minor crisis was over. Mr. Meow promptly jumped up onto my lap, spun around three times before settling into a curled-up ball of fluff, his tiny body vibrating as he purred his happiness.

"Notice anything?" I asked Levi.

"What?"

"You're not sneezing?" I hinted.

"Oh my god, you're right. It worked. You fixed my allergy."

"Happy to help."

Levi's smile slipped, and he put a hand up to his temple, pressing.

"What's wrong?"

"I'm getting a vision." Moving around the sofa, he swept the books off the end and collapsed next to me, his head resting against the back of the couch, eyes closed. Curious, I reached out and took hold of his hand, seeing if I could channel his vision. Turned out I could. We both watched as a slightly hysterical young woman stood at the front counter of the police station, arguing with the officer that her co-worker had been taken over by aliens.

The young woman's name was Lucina, and she was neither lying nor off her meds. She was a bartender at a joint downtown, had a boyfriend who had a penchant for tattoos, and was addicted to cooking shows...though why anyone would be entertained by watching another person cook was beyond me. And she thought her colleague had been taken over by aliens—that was the only explanation for his weird behavior.

"Explain the weird behavior," the officer said. He not only didn't believe her but he wasn't interested at all. His mind was on other things. Like the date he had lined up after work tonight.

"We tend bar in shifts, and Jacob and I are usually rostered on together, so I know him pretty well. But today, he was all over the place. He didn't know how to pull a beer! He didn't know how to use the cash register. It was like he'd never worked behind a bar before. It looked like him, but it wasn't. His body has been taken over. By aliens."

Pushing further into Lucina's psych, I discovered that Lucina was also a massive fan of a television show called *The X-Files* and was obsessed with the idea of life beyond the planet earth. She was right, of course. There was plenty of life beyond this realm— she just didn't know what.

The vision ended. Levi opened his eyes and turned his head to look at me.

"Did you see that?"

"Yes."

"Is it possible the soul stealer has taken possession of Jacob's body?" he asked.

"Possible but unlikely. He was already in human form when he came through. Why take control of someone? Unless he couldn't maintain his human form? That he has to possess an actual human body to maintain his presence here."

"How much do you know about soul stealers?" Levi narrowed his eyes at me, and I shrugged.

"Not a whole lot. They're not from my dimension. Or yours."

"Soooo...you know nothing?" His voice was incredulous.

"I know he's not meant to be here, and I need to send him back. Look, you do realize there is more than one God, right? So, Dad, he created this realm —Earth. Of course, he'd already created Heaven, that's his home, and then, I admit it was an afterthought, he created Hell. We're all his creations in these three realms. Beyond that, the pocket realms and whatever else is out there have all been created by other Gods."

"Ha!" Levi practically fist-pumped the air, and I knew I'd given him the answer that had been puzzling him for quite some time. He was silent for a moment, then asked, "How do you know it needs the souls of the other two girls to stay here?"

"It's like a download. When I touched Emily, I got traces of him, what he is, what he's after."

"Why is he here? Is he a he?"

"He took male form, so I assume he's a male. And I don't know why he's here."

"Why not?"

I shrugged. "Because I couldn't read that from him. Just that he feeds on souls, and he needs Sarah's and Brianna's to enable him to stay here. I don't know why he wanted to come here or why he wants to stay. We need to catch up with him and find out. And send him back."

"You want to go check out this bar, see if the girl's story pans out?" Levi asked.

"Definitely." Our hands were still linked, and Levi stood, pulling me to my feet, dislodging Mr. Meow, who grumbled in protest, then promptly curled up into a ball where I'd been sitting and fell back to sleep. I tamped down the heady feeling of Levi's hand in mine. We had work to do.

CHAPTER

SEVEN

The Black Swan was on the outskirts of town, the fading light enough to highlight the peeling paint and unkempt appearance. The parking lot was unpaved, simply a pothole expanse of dirt. Several pickups and motorbikes were parked haphazardly. Levi pulled up to the curb, electing not to partake of the bar's car parking facilities. I couldn't blame him. Some of those potholes looked waist-deep.

Climbing out of the car, I stood and looked at the bar—I had a feeling many of the souls inside would be visiting me in the future, and I wondered if there were any I could save now. Doubtful, but I was compelled to try. I pushed out my senses to see if I could feel the soul stealer but detected nothing. I wanted to stamp my foot in frustration but didn't.

"Coming?" Levi asked. He'd already rounded the hood of his van and had taken several steps across the parking lot before realizing I was still standing beside the vehicle. Shaking off my thoughts, I gave him a nod and stepped onto the parking lot.

Pain ricocheted up my legs, and my feet burned as if they were in the fires of Hell, which was saying something because Hellfire did not burn me. I yelped and jumped back.

"Lucy?" Levi turned, puzzled.

"I can't cross the lot," I told him, gingerly dipping my toe into the parking lot only to quickly withdraw it when another jolt shot through me. "Someone has warded it."

"Warded it? Why hasn't it stopped me?"

"Because it's not for humans. It's to keep out paranormals. Although it may not be aimed at me specifically until I break the ward, I can't come in." I squinted at the bar, trying to identify any hidden symbols. There had to be symbols somewhere for the ward to work. If I could find one, I could have Levi break its lines, rendering the ward void. Only I couldn't see one. Whoever had set this up was smart, and I was grateful we hadn't driven into the parking lot—I'd have been a writhing mass of agony by now if that had been the case.

Standing on the edge of the parking lot, I moved my hands in the air, drawing glowing red symbols as I worked at breaking the ward. It only took a couple of minutes, and Levi was standing there watching, fascinated. With a satisfied smile, I stepped onto the parking lot, pausing for a moment to check. Nope, no burning sensation, no pain.

I was three steps in when spirits began rising from the ground. What on earth was going on here? Why were there ghosts in the parking lot of a bar? Was this…hallowed ground? An old cemetery? The ghosts were multiplying, too many to count. But hallowed ground made no sense; hallowed ground wouldn't keep me out. And I very much doubted the citizens of Shadow Falls would build a bar on top of a cemetery.

I took another two steps when they attacked. Hands grabbed and scratched at me, and one woman managed to sink her teeth into my shoulder before I could push her off. Interesting how they were corporeal when they touched me, meaning they could inflict pain. And they were fast, faster than rats on a sinking ship. I'd throw one off, and another ten would take its place.

I could easily blast them out of existence in one fell swoop, but I didn't want to destroy them. They'd been human once. They deserved their chance at Heaven. Or Hell. I'd much rather call a reaper and send them on their way, but if they forced the issue, I'd have no choice but to destroy them. And that didn't sit well with me.

It wasn't until I heard Levi grunt that I realized he, too, was being attacked. The flare of concern overwhelmed me, and I reacted instinctively, red beams shooting across the parking lot as I blasted the ghosts that had already tackled Levi to the ground. I quickly drew a symbol, encasing Levi in a protective box. The spirits banged their fists against it, trying to get to him.

My distraction with Levi cost me: I was covered in mindless zombie ghosts, dragged to the ground where we rolled. It crossed my mind that I'd destroyed some of them to save Levi, but I held back from doing the same to protect myself. My concern for him was greater than my concern for myself. Being on Earth was so confusing. Being attracted to a human even more so.

I kicked and thrashed at the zombie ghosts, who were intent on one thing. Me. But they couldn't really harm me. Yes, their bites hurt, but I healed immediately. All they were doing was slowing me down. That was when realization dawned. Someone wanted to slow me down, stop me from entering the bar. Holy shit. The soul stealer must be in there. I struggled harder against the ghosts, but my own agitation appeared to fuel them, for suddenly, they were stronger. How was this happening? It made no sense. A big burly ghost sat on me, knocking the air from my lungs.

"Just kill them, Lucy." Dacian's voice. I turned my head, peered through the limbs of the ghosts, and caught a glimpse of him leaning against Levi's van, watching with arms crossed over his chest.

"No. It's not their fault. They're being controlled. I need to break it." I grunted as someone bit my thigh, then my calf. They clearly weren't above fighting dirty. I managed to throw a few more off, but as soon as I got rid of one, two returned to replace them. They'd piled onto my legs so I could no longer kick. One arm was trapped under four bodies, but I still had my left arm, and I was afraid Dacian was right. Would I have to kill them, extinguish their souls forever to stop this madness? Still, I hesitated, and it cost me. I'd assumed they didn't have weapons, but a searing pain in my ribs had me screaming in agony.

Fire burned through my lungs, and I glanced down to see a sword plunged into my side. *What the fuck?* This wasn't right. Confusion slowed my thought processes, and I feared I'd left it too late. Dacian was right. I had to kill them. Lifting my arm, I threw out a red bolt, catching three ghosts and evaporating them instantly. But I was weakening. Blood was flowing from the wound in my side, and my head was spinning. Every living creature could die, including immortals. You just needed the right weapon. It appeared the ghosts had the right weapon. The question was, what was it, and how did they get it? Because this sword wasn't your average sword, of that, I was certain.

Suddenly a blinding light shot out, and I flung my arm over my eyes.

"You're hurt." Dacian was kneeling by my side, a frown on his face. I let my arm drop from my face and looked at him. My friend from old. The one who now hated me and didn't remember me at all. Yet he'd just eradicated every single ghost. All that remained? The sword still embedded in my side.

"Could you?" I nodded at the sword, and Dacian grabbed it and pulled it out with little regard for the slicing of my internal organs. I couldn't contain my yelp. *By Hell, that stings.* I closed my eyes and concentrated on healing myself. The sword had gone deep, torn through some organs that I needed, but within seconds I was healed.

"Care to tell me what that was all about?" Dacian asked, rising to his feet and backing away from me. The sword dangled from his hand, covered in my blood, but beneath the blood, it glowed.

"I have no idea." I eyed the sword. Where had it come from? "Can I see?" I indicated the sword, but Dacian lifted it over his shoulder and tucked it into the scabbard I knew he carried on his back, hidden beneath his wings.

"Think I'll keep this. Looks like it might come in handy."

"Come on, Dacian, you and I both know you're not going to kill me. You had the perfect opportunity just then, and you didn't take it."

"I still need answers. I cannot get them from you if you are dead."

"What answers?"

"Why you unleashed an otherworld creature on Earth, for starters."

"I told you," I cried in exasperation, "it wasn't me. This soul stealer is from a pocket dimension. He got through because the veil is thin right now. It's All Hallows' Eve, remember?"

"Why don't I believe you?"

"I don't lie, Dacian, you know that. Rather than wasting your time on me, you should be helping me catch the soul stealer. After all, it was most likely Michael and Gabriel who are behind all of this in the first place."

"They would do no such thing. They're not the bad guys." Dacian stiffened, and his fingers clenched and unclenched. Yeah, right. Then why did I get prior notice in Hell of Emily's death? Someone knew it was coming. Someone sent me a message. If not my brothers, who? While the girls may have opened the portal during their séance, I suspected my brothers of planting the idea in their heads. Compelling humans was easy; any angel could do it. I was about to explain my theory to Dacian when Levi shouted my name.

With a wave of my hand, the invisible box surrounding him disappeared. He was pointing at the bar, and now I could hear it—shouting and the sounds of a fight. Levi ran toward the door, and I followed close behind.

Tables were overturned, and chairs were broken. Someone was unconscious on the floor with a man standing over him. The black hooded cloak looked familiar.

Levi skidded to a halt, and I bumped into his back. Silently I moved to his side, standing ever so slightly in front of him. The guy in the cloak glanced from Levi to me, and as our gazes met, I saw what looked like galaxies swirling in his eyes.

"It's him," I breathed, keeping my voice low. "He's the soul stealer."

"Fucking great," Levi whispered, lips barely moving. I went to step forward, but Levi's hand snaked out and gripped my wrist, holding me in place. I ignored the pleasant tingle from the flesh-on-flesh contact and kept my eyes trained on the soul stealer.

"Who are you?" I asked. I'd pushed out my senses but couldn't get a read on who or what he was. He had power, I knew that much. I was kicking myself for underestimating him; it was a rookie mistake, and I should have known better. My brothers would have a field day with this, but maybe that had been their intention all along.

"Zuska." As he spoke, I caught a glimpse of his teeth. Pointy. And lots of them. Two rows from what I could see. Yet when I'd seen him take Emily's soul, he hadn't bitten her. He'd dragged her soul from her through a kiss. So why all the teeth? And his skin was pale, more gray than anything.

"Is that your name or species?" I pushed. If I could find out what he was, I could find out how to defeat him—that is, if I couldn't get him back through the portal and back to his own dimension.

"Enough talk, Devil." His voice was flat, devoid of emotion.

"You know me?" No surprise. My brothers had set this up, probably given him all the intel he needed on me. Not only did it piss me off, but it riled me that I was on the defensive, that I was in the dark with what I was dealing with. But since when had my brothers ever fought fair?

The man on the ground groaned, drawing our attention. Zuska bent slightly toward him, and Levi shouted, "Back off, mother fucker, or I will blow your goddamn head off!" I quickly glanced at him. Did he have a gun?

It all happened so fast. A flash of anger on Zuska's face. We'd interrupted his snack. He drew back his arm, and I saw the bolt of energy leave his palm, aimed for Levi. I stepped in front of Levi. Swiveling to face him, I extended my wings and cocooned us with them. The energy bolt bounced off, doing no harm.

"He's gone." I felt the void of Zuska's energy. So

he didn't want a confrontation. Or he didn't want it here and now? I wondered why.

"Lucy?" Levi's voice was strangled.

"Yes, Levi?"

"What. The. Hell?"

I cleared my throat. "So, these are my wings, and they come in handy as a shield if I'm not using them for flying," I explained.

"They're...on fire," Levi squeaked, and I finally noticed he was standing ramrod straight, barely breathing.

"Relax, they won't burn you. Only if I want them to. Which I don't. See?" Before he could stop me, I moved the tip of my wing and lightly caressed his cheek. He sucked in a breath and closed his eyes, and I imagined he was waiting for the pain. Which didn't come, of course. Slowly his eyes opened, and he looked at me in wonder. We stood pressed together, and I became aware of his heat, his delicious scent that set my heart racing and gave me thoughts I had no business thinking over a human. He broke the spell before I could muster the will to do so.

"You're hurt!" He pushed me back, and I retracted my wings, staggering slightly. Levi put his hands on my shoulders to steady me as his eyes took in my torn T-shirt and the bloodstain that soaked the fabric.

"I'm fine," I reassured him. "All healed. See?" I lifted my shirt and showed him my side. I jumped slightly when his hand reached out and traced across my flesh.

"Only God can judge me," he muttered. He was reading the words inked along my rib. I'd gotten the tattoo on a dare from Michael and Gabriel. I think they'd been hoping I'd get something embarrassing or cliché, but when they'd seen it, they'd been green with envy. Always one step behind, my brothers.

"You need to get cleaned up." Levi moved his hand away, and I looked down at the tacky blood staining my skin.

"Let me deal with this lot first." The patrons in the bar were looking at us in astonishment.

"What are you going to do?"

"Just a little memory adjustment. They'll think there was a brawl. They'll forget about Zuska and us. But if you don't want to be affected, I'd step outside," I told him.

"Right." He hightailed it out the door, and I allowed myself a moment to admire his tight ass encased in denim. He wore it well.

Closing my eyes, I called on my power and

adjusted the memories of everyone in the room. It took but a second, but I felt light-headed and a little wobbly on my feet once I was done. I'd used a lot of power today, and I was starting to feel the effects. I didn't recharge as quickly as if I'd been home. Earth's dimension was draining.

Stepping outside, I shivered in the evening air. It was dark now. The parking lot looked just as it had when we arrived, with no sign of the spirits and the fight that had unfolded. Dacian was gone too, and I wondered why he hadn't come into the bar. He said he was also searching for Zuska, the soul stealer, and it crossed my mind that maybe that wasn't his true purpose. I felt a twinge in my chest at the hurt that flared when I thought about his hatred toward me. Why had he turned against me, and why couldn't he remember our past? Zuska was my first priority, but Dacian was definitely my second. I had to get things straightened out with him.

EIGHT

"Lucy?" Levi gave my shoulder a nudge, and I jerked awake. Blinking away my fatigue, I turned to face him.

"Wha?"

"You okay?" The concern in his voice touched me.

"Used too much power today," I grunted, fumbling for the door handle and practically falling out of the vehicle.

"Wait, I'll help you."

Ignoring him, I managed to get my feet under me and glance around. We were in the parking lot behind Levi's shop.

"Let's get inside. You're freezing." It was true.

Clad in my ripped T-shirt that was soggy with my blood, I'd started to shiver. I could easily conjure myself a change of clothes or a warm coat, but I was concerned with how low my energy reserves were. Something was wrong. Had the sword done more damage than I thought? Had I not healed properly? It made sense to conserve what energy I had left, so I let my body shiver and shake, knowing Levi would take care of me.

Once I'd dragged myself up the stairs and into Levi's apartment, I headed toward the sofa. I was about to collapse onto it when he snagged an arm around my waist and pulled me up against him.

"No getting blood on my sofa," he grumbled. "Shower first. I'll get you something to wear."

"You have women's clothes here?" I couldn't keep the surprise from my voice.

"No. You can wear something of mine. It'll be too big, but it'll do for sleeping in. I can put your stuff through the wash."

"Don't bother. Once I'm rested and have my energy back, I can conjure up some clothes. But right now, I'm exhausted, no can do."

I could see on his face that he wanted to ask me about the conjuring thing, but he let it drop, instead leading me to the bathroom. Reaching into the shower, he flicked the tap on, then glanced at me. "You okay to take it from here?"

"Why? You offering to strip me naked and wash me?" I couldn't stop the image my own words planted in my mind and the heat that speared through my body in response. He ignored me. "Yell out if you need anything."

Brushing past me, he closed the bathroom door behind him. With a sigh, I stripped out of my clothes, leaving them in a heap on the floor. I adjusted the temperature, then stood beneath the spray. The water flowed red, washing away the blood. I looked at my side, where the glowing sword had pierced me, and frowned. There was a mark. A scar. I didn't scar. Was it because of all the energy I'd expelled fighting the zombie ghosts? Breaking the ward? Doing the mind wipe on all the humans? But that was small stuff. I shouldn't be this exhausted. I could barely keep my eyes open, and even though the water pounding down on me was blissful, I simply stood beneath the spray, too drained to actually wash.

After a while, there was a bang on the door, and Levi asking if I was okay. I roused myself. I do believe I'd been dozing, standing upright in the shower.

"Yeah," I replied, flipping off the tap and stepping out of the shower. I grabbed one of the giant gray towels hanging on the towel rack and wrapped it around myself before opening the door. Levi had one hand planted against the frame, leaning against it.

"You look…" He trailed off.

"Better?" I supplied helpfully.

"Like a drowned rat." His lips curled in a grin, but I didn't have the energy to respond. Fuck me, something was really wrong here, and I felt a twinge of panic. Was I dying? Seeing my face, Levi immediately sobered.

"What's wrong?" he demanded, straightening from his casual lean against the doorframe.

"I think something's wrong. With me. I think I'm hurt."

"What? Where?" His eyes devoured me from head to toe, looking for signs of injury, but standing there clutching the towel to my chest was tiring. Everything was tiring. Breathing was tiring. My eyes fluttered closed, and I felt Levi catch me against his chest, swearing.

"Lucy? What's going on?" Suddenly the world

tilted as he swung me up into his arms. I wished I had the energy to enjoy being so close to him, but alas, I could feel myself slipping into oblivion—I just hoped it wasn't forever, that I'd recover from this. Otherwise, my brothers had won, and the Earth was doomed.

"GOOD MORNING!" Levi smiled as he bustled around the kitchen. He was dressed in his usual jeans and T-shirt. Only his feet were bare. I liked the domesticated look on him.

"Ummm. What happened?" I'd woken in a strange bed, still wrapped in a towel, another wrapped haphazardly around my head.

"Ah, I wondered if you'd remember passing out last night." Levi turned, spatula in hand. "You were exhausted, passed out in my arms, slept like the dead all night. I thought the smell of me cooking breakfast might be enough to draw you out."

"I'm starving." And I was. My stomach was doing the growling thing again. "You stayed with me?" I asked.

"You said you were hurt. I was worried, so I put you in my bed. Meant to check on you throughout the night, but I fell asleep too. You were still breathing when I woke up this morning, so I figured you were okay. You'd wake up when you were ready." He paused, looking me up and down.

"You wear a towel well." He nodded at the towel still wrapped around my body. The one in my hair had fallen loose as soon as I'd gotten out of bed, and my hair was a mass of tangles around my head. I'd been too intent on finding Levi that I hadn't bothered to dress. With a flick of my hand, I remedied that situation. Jeans, boots, a dusky rose blouse, and a snug leather jacket. My hair once more tangle-free; it fell in shiny black waves down my back.

Sliding onto a bar stool at the kitchen counter, I watched as Levi made me a coffee, sliding the steaming mug toward me before he turned his attention back to whatever was cooking on the stove. I took a sip of the hot brew, closing my eyes with appreciation. I'd developed an addiction to coffee the first time I'd tasted it, back in the ninth century when a goat herder discovered the benefits of the beans when his goats ate them off the coffee plant. There was such a fuss that I'd visited Earth to partake of this strange new beverage and had been hooked ever since.

"So last night at the bar," Levi began, "and the soul stealer. He didn't possess anyone's body, right? I mean, he looked the same to me, even though I didn't really see him up close before."

"No, he didn't possess anyone."

"So the vision with Lucina? A dead end?"

"I think you picked up on her energy, her true belief that something terrible had happened to her friend." That was why Levi had the vision—anyone sending out powerful energy spikes like that would be bound to trigger him.

"Aliens then?"

"Not aliens. Twins. Her colleague, the one she thought was acting strangely, has an identical twin. Only Lucina didn't know that, just that he had a brother. They pulled a prank, switching places." I'd pieced it together last night. The whole scenario had revealed itself to me when I'd placed my hand on the wooden surface of the bar.

"So it was purely coincidence that we go to that particular bar to check it out, and soul stealer is there? About to take a soul?"

"Perhaps not a coincidence. A connection, a small thread for us to follow."

"And what about the parking lot? All those spirits, attacking us. And you were hurt."

"I don't know what that was about," I admitted. "The soul stealer is more powerful than I gave him credit for, and if he's controlling spirits and giving them weapons to use against me, then..."

"Then what?"

"I need to be very, very careful." I thought again of the sword piercing my side, the pain like nothing I'd ever felt before. The mark on my flesh that hadn't healed. Hiking my shirt up, I looked at my side to see if I'd finished healing during the night.

"That looks...painful." Levi peered at the scar still marring my skin, and I took a closer look. It was still the light pink of last night. The puckered edges hadn't disappeared at all. I touched it. No pain. No tenderness.

"I've been on Earth before and never had such a reaction, such exhaustion," I explained, smoothing my shirt back down. "I think it has something to do with the sword and my injury. Perhaps it took more energy than I realized to heal myself—it went in deep."

"And it's scarred. Is that normal?"

"No." I pushed down my worry, not wanting Levi to realize what a big deal this was.

Levi looked at me but didn't say anything more. "Here, get this into you. Maybe you just need some fuel." Placing a plate piled high with bacon, eggs, hash browns, fried tomatoes, and toast in front of me, he slid onto the stool next to me, watching as I ate.

"Aren't you eating?" I asked through a mouthful.

"Already eaten. I've been trying to channel Sarah and Brianna, get a feel for where they are, how they're doing."

"Any luck?"

"Yes, but get this—I'm pretty sure they went to school today."

"You think that's strange?" I quirked an eyebrow.

"Well, their best friend just died. I wouldn't expect them to go to school. Not until after the funeral, at least, and that is probably a few days away."

Levi had a point. The teenage girls had a get-out-of-school-free card. Why would they go to school when they didn't have to? Unless they weren't at the school?

"Take my hand." I held out my hand, palm up, to Levi. He placed his hand in mine without question.

"What are we doing?" he asked.

"Channeling them. I want to use your powers, help boost your connection to them."

"Do you think something is wrong?"

"Not necessarily, but you're right. It's odd that they're at school. I just want to check that they are at school and not somewhere else."

"Okay." He closed his eyes in concentration, and I allowed Levi's energy to blend with mine. I zeroed in on the connection with the talismans. Closing my own eyes, I watched the scene unfold. There they were, Sarah and Brianna, and yes, they were definitely at school, talking to each other while Brianna retrieved something—a workbook—from her locker. I broke the connection and looked at Levi.

"Did you see?"

"That was...amazing. I've never had a vision so clear. It was like watching television."

I grinned. "Pretty neat, huh? But back to the point. The girls are at school. Sitting ducks for the soul stealer. He can easily trace their old energy, and at the school, those remnants of energy would be very concentrated. He'd know they frequent that place a lot. He only has to wait to know they'd turn up there eventually."

"Shit." Levi ran a hand over his face. "Do you think he knows? Senses them?"

I shook my head. "Not yet. He can't sense them,

remember? So he'd have to physically go and check it out and see if he can find them. Maybe he's already done that today and missed them. But we need to get over there before he can get to them." I kept the concern from my voice. It would be bad, very bad if the soul stealer caught up with them.

Levi had been right. Once I'd eaten and had a coffee, I felt one hundred percent my old self. I'd stolen a glimpse to see if the scar still marred my skin on the way out to the van and tamped down my worry that while the scar had faded from pink to a thin white line, it was still a scar. Don't get me wrong, I wasn't precious about having flawless skin. I was worried about why I was scarred. Ordinarily, you could slice my hand off, and it would grow back with no signs of injury. But this? This was different, another complication to add to my worries Earthside.

In the confines of the van, it was impossible to ignore Levi by my side. He smelled so damn delicious I wanted to lean over and taste him with my tongue. It confused me, the heady emotions of being close to him, of the overwhelming *hunger* I experienced whenever I was within his orbit. It made me wriggle in my seat, drawing attention to myself.

"Everything okay?" He'd put sunglasses on, and I could see myself reflected in the lenses. I nodded. *Fine. Everything was fine.* I conjured my own sunglasses to hide behind.

I listened to his inane chatter as we headed out to the school. He told me about the town and its history, how it was founded in the mining era, how he'd moved here after his grandmother had died. My heart melted a little when I realized he'd been caring for his grandmother, that he'd seen to her every need until she'd passed. That said a lot about a man. That was back in Redmeadows. She'd taught him the craft, had recognized the signs of clairvoyance in him and had nurtured them, and kudos to her, she'd taught him well.

"Sorry. I must be boring you." Levi laughed self-deprecatingly, and I shook my head in denial.

"Not at all. Your grandmother sounds like a wonderful lady. I'm sorry for your loss." For I could feel it, beneath his words and memories and recollections was the thread of pain for what was gone.

"She was." He glanced my way. Taking one hand off the wheel, he reached over and placed his hand over mine, where it rested on my thigh. The untamed bolt of desire was volatile, scorching me with the fierceness of it.

I cleared my throat. "And your parents? Are they in Redmeadows?"

He removed his hand, placing it back on the wheel, and I missed his touch. He nodded. "Yeah. They don't necessarily approve of my career choice. Mom wanted me to follow my love of food and be a chef or something. Dad wanted me to follow him into corporate. Neither of those paths was the right one for me, and of course, Grandma had my back. She helped me set up Black Hat."

Ah, the logo of the woman in the long dress and parasol was a nod to his grandmother. I approved. "That was generous of her. And difficult, knowing she was going against her own daughter's wishes for you."

"I guess." He shrugged. "The store in Redmeadows was small. Tiny. And I did readings mostly. We didn't have money for much stock, and I needed to build up my clientele and credibility."

"Your grandmother did readings too." That's why he'd left. When she died, he could feel her presence in the store as if she were physically there, sitting at her velvet-covered table, reading a client's palm. And it hurt him. The memories were painful. So he'd packed up his shop and moved to Shadow Falls. I felt all of it as he talked about his past, then laughed again, apologizing for going on about it. This time I reached out and placed my hand on his arm.

"It's okay. You need to talk, and I need to listen." We all have our roles in this life, and at this moment in time, this was mine. To listen as he told me his story. No judgment, no fixing anything. Just listen. And try not to let myself be distracted by how much I wanted him.

We lapsed into silence, each lost in our own thoughts until he pulled into the school parking lot and killed the engine.

"Lucy..." Pushing his glasses to the top of his head, he rested a forearm across the steering wheel as he turned to face me. The light caught his eyes, making the flecks of gold brighter, dragging me in until I was drowning in the depths of them.

"Yes?" I kept my glasses in place, hiding my eyes

from him, hiding the lust that was surely burning in my own.

He raised a hand to my face, tracing from cheekbone to jaw with his fingertips. A deep hunger flashed in his irises, and my body responded in kind, a warmth flooding my abdomen.

A thud against the windscreen had both our heads snapping around. A ball bounced away, a young boy grinning sheepishly and calling out "sorry" as he retrieved the ball. Clearing my throat, I muttered, "We'd better get moving. Find Sarah and Brianna."

"Right." We climbed out of the van, doors slamming simultaneously. That was when it hit me. A tsunami of guilt, worry, fear, arrogance, evil. The vibration of hundreds of school kids, some good, some not. I wanted to hunt down the bullies, the cheats, the mean kids, and set them straight, for this was where it started, this was where evil got a foothold and grew like mold in a damp basement. Shaking off the sensations bombarding me, I followed Levi, who was heading toward a building named "Administration."

"Wait!" I caught up with him. "What are you doing?"

"Going to the admin building. They can tell us what classes Sarah and Brianna are in."

I shook my head. "We can find them ourselves through the talismans. Plus, I don't want others involved in this. The more people involved, the more complicated it gets, and a higher risk that something could go wrong."

"What do you mean?" He stopped, and I nearly bumped into him.

"We go in there and ask where the girls are. They want to know why. They may or may not give us that information—I'd say not since we're not their parents and we're not law enforcement. So then they're suspicious. What are we doing? They start asking questions. Digging. Drawing attention."

"Aaah. Gotcha. But...if we're walking around the school, aren't we going to be noticed? Isn't someone, at some point, going to question what we're doing here?"

"I'm going to use a light compulsion so that we won't be noticed. We'll be seen, but not noticed. But stay close to me, okay? I can't stretch it too far."

"Fucking awesome." He grinned. "This is fucking awesome."

I let Levi use his skills to track the talismans. Just like a muscle, magic had to be practiced and used to strengthen it. The more Levi used his magic, the stronger it would become. It was rare for a human to have such abilities, and I knew that I'd have to teach him how to mask his magic so others couldn't exploit it.

We found ourselves in a wide corridor, lockers on either side. One locker on the left was decorated with hearts and cards, and on the floor in front of it, lots and lots of flowers and a candle or two. Emily's locker. The students had made a memorial of it.

"They're coming this way," Levi told me. "Their energy is really strong and getting stronger."

"Good work." I grabbed hold of his hand to stop him. We'd wait here. Let them come to us. If Emily's locker was here, then Sarah's and Brianna's weren't far away. Sure enough, a bell rang, and the hallway was flooded with students. I pulled us off to the side, next to Emily's locker, and waited.

They rounded the corner, linked arm in arm. As they drew closer, I knew why they were here. The attention. Sarah loved the attention. Brianna, not so much, but she didn't want to be alone. I paused for a moment, letting my attention settle on Sarah to get a better read on her. She was a people pleaser, would go along with almost anything to keep everyone else happy. She wanted a career in medicine. She often had a distorted view of what was right—in her quest to make everyone happy, she often did the wrong thing...either for herself or her friends.

Interesting. I could feel the discord in her. Her grief over the loss of Emily, but her delight at being the center of attention because of it. This was new for her, I realized. In the past, she'd been in the background, always putting everyone else before herself, so she didn't get the attention she secretly craved.

Switching my attention to Brianna, I read her too, wincing slightly at what I discovered. She had many scars from her youth and didn't trust easily, but she would do anything for her best friends. Emily and Sarah. Brianna had a smart head on her shoulders and a strong personality. She knew how to stand up for herself and had plans for a career in politics.

"Ladies." Stepping forward, I dropped the compulsion enough so that they were aware of me. Surprise crossed their faces, and I smiled. "You both must be exemplary students, coming to school the day after your friend was killed."

Guilt not only flashed across their faces, but it also swarmed their auras like a heavy fog.

"I guess I didn't explain myself clearly enough when we gave you those talismans." Nodding at their wrists, I continued, "But the creature that killed Sarah? It wants you. And while those bracelets will help stop it from finding you, if it is here, waiting, and sees you? You're toast."

I turned to Levi. "Did that make sense to you? I mean, was I clear? Because I'm not sure they're getting it."

"Sounded clear enough to me." Levi nodded. "Girls? Make sense to you?"

"You said it would hide us," Sarah said, twisting the bracelet on her arm.

"I also said to stay put. Keep a low profile. This soul stealer needs both of your souls to make his stay here permanent. We need to stop that from happening. The bracelet doesn't make you invisible. It just stops him from tracing your energy. So please, for all that is holy, go home. Stay there. Inside."

"We will. Come on, Sarah, let's get out of here. I knew this was a bad idea." Grabbing Sarah's hand, Brianna dragged her away.

"Do we follow them?" Levi asked, watching the girls scurry off down the hallway.

"Nah. I've got something else here I need to take care of. I'll meet you by the van."

"Oh?"

"Nothing for you to worry about, Levi. Wait outside for me. I'll only be a few minutes."

Sensing he was going to argue with me, I pushed a little compulsion his way and waited until he was out of view before hunting down English teacher Ray Blinds. His energy had been niggling at me ever since I'd stepped foot in this building, and I couldn't leave without paying him a little visit. I found him in his classroom, flicking through his phone as his students scribbled madly at their desks.

His head snapped around as I walked in, and I made sure I was fully visible to him but shielded from the students, who didn't react to my presence whatsoever.

"Ray Blinds." It wasn't a question.

"Who are you? What are you doing here? We're in the middle of a test." His belligerent tone irked me.

"Relax, they don't know I'm here." I sat on the corner of his desk and looked at him. A middle-aged man, overweight, hated his job, hated his life, and took it out on his wife in repeated drunken rages. He opened his mouth to speak, but I shushed him.

"Listen up, Ray, it's your lucky day because most people like you don't get this warning. Usually, you turn up to the gates of Hell and meet me there. I'm giving you the opportunity to redeem yourself before that happens."

"What the fuck are you talking about?"

"Ray! Language, there are children present." I laughed at the sudden panic emanating from him as he looked beyond me to his students. Tempting as it was to play this game with him, I knew Levi was waiting outside for me, so I had to hurry it along. Leaning forward, I placed my hand on his head and played him a compilation of his own memories, of all the times he'd hit his wife, of her screams, her cries, and his indifference.

"See that shit there, Ray? That's what earns you a spot in Hell. I mean, right now, at this point in time, you wouldn't be in the pit, but you'd be in a cell enduring eternal torture. Like what, you ask? Oh, things like, let me see, being beaten daily by demons—only to heal and have it start all over again the next day. No? Doesn't appeal? What about having your hands cut off? Not just the once, mind you. We're about eternal damnation. We'd cut them off, wait for them to grow back—because we can do that in Hell—and then cut them off again. Do you recognize a theme here, Ray?"

He gulped, paling, but I wasn't finished. "And if

you killed her, Ray? If you went too far? That would get you into the pit. The fire pit. Where you will burn, forever. No healing, no reprieve, just your flesh melting from your bones over and over. You open your mouth to scream, and flames crawl down your throat, burning your lungs, consuming you from the inside out. Sound like a good time, Ray?"

He shook his head, terror in his eyes.

"You know who I am, Ray?" I leaned forward, my face inches from his, letting him see the Hellfire burning in my eyes.

"You're Satan," he whispered.

"I prefer Lucifer, but damn straight I am." Straightening, I slid off his desk and moved behind him, tracing my fingers across his shoulders, a black mist following, feeling him shudder. "Here's what's going to happen, Ray, my man. You are going to give up the booze. Starting now. Ditch the flask in your drawer, the bottle in your glove box, and that bar you have set up at home? Tonight you take a sledgehammer to it. You will apologize to your wife and mean it. You will woo her and love her like you did when you proposed, for Lord help her, she still loves you. You will never raise a hand, or even your voice, to her ever again. You're unhappy with your life, with your job? That's not her fault. You're not a tree. Fucking move. Do something about it. Take that course you've been thinking about. Become a counselor. Take control and take accountability."

"I will," he whispered, throat clogged with emotion.

"And remember this, Raymond, when your time on Earth is up, and your spirit crosses, I will know, and I will come for you. Or not. Let's hope we don't meet again, eh?"

Patting him on the shoulder, I sauntered out of the classroom, confident Ray Blinds was on a new path.

TEN

It was two days with zero action. The first day I spent with Levi, hanging out in his shop, watching as he did readings and impressed me all over again with his skills. I wondered if he knew his grandmother was here. She stood behind him, several feet away, as if knowing that if she moved closer, he'd sense her. The way he'd talked about her, I got the impression he didn't realize she visited him. The minute the thought entered my mind that I should ask him, her hazel eyes clashed with mine, and she shook her head. I decided to leave it be. After all, it wasn't my business.

The second day I ventured out alone. Strolling through Shadow Falls Square, I'd stopped and listened in when three old men, sitting at a bus stop, were reminiscing about the old days. The old days where they'd planned heists. I would have crossed to them then and there and tagged them for Hell if I hadn't known the truth. That the heists were always foiled before they got off the ground, for all three men had a weakness for the ladies. They'd start casing a joint, but the eye candy was too distracting, and they couldn't get themselves organized enough to follow through. I couldn't hold back the laugh at their plight. Each man had married one of the girls from the three heists they'd intended to pull off. The women had unwittingly stopped them from a life of crime.

I also noticed that everywhere I went, Dacian followed. He kept his distance, and I was done chasing him for answers. I couldn't control what he thought of me, even though it was wrong. I'd tried to convince him of my good intentions, tried to get him to remember our past, but he was too stubborn to believe me. Plus, I had more important things to worry about.

The soul stealer had gone quiet. I knew he was here somewhere—I could feel him, like a tiny splinter buried under your skin that you can't quite get a grip on to pull out. And this particular splinter was in my side, where the glowing sword had sliced into me. My best guess was the sword belonged to the soul stealer. He'd left it with the zombie ghosts to use against me. Which meant he must have another weapon, a more potent weapon in case the sword failed. Yet the energy bolt he threw at us at the bar was powerless against me, so why hadn't he used his backup weapon? Getting a feel for my strengths and weaknesses, perhaps?

I'd considered going back to Hell to instruct Ashliel into doing some research, but I was reluctant to leave this realm, even for a quick trip home. As soon as I did, the humans would be vulnerable. It had nothing to do with my desire not to leave Levi's side. Nothing at all.

"All that frowning will give you wrinkles." Dacian fell into step beside me, and I glanced at him out of the corner of my eye.

"Unlikely, but thanks for the concern." We continued the walk in silence. It was a beautiful spring day, white puffy clouds in the sky, warm enough to take off your jacket and enjoy the sunshine. I sat on a bench and did just that. Tilting my head back, I basked in the glow of the sun. I felt Dacian sit next to me but didn't bother opening my eyes.

"Why are you here?" I asked him.

"I told you—" he began, but I cut him off.

"No. Today. Here. Now. Why are you here now?"

I heard the rustle of his clothing, guessed he had shrugged his shoulders. Tilting my head, I squinted one eye open to look at him. He had one arm stretched out along the bench, his hand inches from my hair. He was looking at me.

"Sorry, I didn't catch that." I grinned. He smiled in return, the first smile since he'd been here, and it reminded me of old times.

"I don't know," he admitted. "You're stubborn and a pain in my ass, and you don't do what I'd expect. You're an enigma, and I can't fucking work you out."

"You know me, Dacian. It's in that thick head of yours somewhere. I wish I knew what my brothers did to you so I could undo it."

"Why do you think they did something to me? Because you think you're so unforgettable?" It was back. The snark. I sighed, closing my eyes again.

"I'm not saying we had an epic love affair. We were friends for a very long time. You trained me to fight. We have a lot of memories together. It makes no sense that you can't recall a single one."

He was silent, and I didn't push. You could lead a horse to water and all that.

"What you're doing here?" he finally said. "Guiding souls onto the right path, steering them from evil. That's...admirable."

"Thanks." Not bothering to open my eyes, I asked, "Does this mean you believe me when I say I'm *not* evil?"

"Maybe." His reluctance was palpable, but I'd take what I could get at this point. We were making progress. He was sitting by my side, and we were having a conversation rather than fighting each other. Which reminded me.

"Do you still have the sword? The one the zombie ghosts had?"

Barking out a laugh, he shifted his hand, touching my hair. "Zombie ghosts?" I kept still, feeling his fingers thread through the strands before sliding free. Then he leaned forward, resting his elbows on his knees and studying the ground in front of him.

"I have *never* had a ghost bite me before," I said defensively. "Zombie ghosts fit. And stop avoiding the question—do you have the sword or not?" If he'd given it to my brothers...well, I wasn't sure what I'd do about it, besides being pissed off.

"I have it. Why?"

"Because it did this." I jumped up, positioned

myself in front of him, and lifted my shirt to reveal the thin white scar. He reached his hand out to trace it, but I backed away. I didn't want his touch—this wasn't the Dacian I remembered.

"You didn't heal." His dark eyes met mine, puzzled.

I shook my head. "Not properly. I mean, I'm okay now, it's all good, but the scar never went away."

"Interesting." His hand reached up to his shoulder, and I hurriedly stepped backward, worried he was going to draw the sword and use it against me. Instead, he rubbed his hand around the back of his neck and sighed. "You think it was the sword?"

"What else could it be? The only reason my tattoo stuck is because of the enchantment we put in the ink. And believe me, it hurt like a son of a bitch getting that done."

"You screamed and screamed and begged him to stop," Dacian murmured absently. I froze. He remembered. He remembered me getting the tattoo. I didn't say a word, didn't want to make a big deal of it, but maybe, just maybe, now that he was away from the influence of my brothers, his memories would return.

"Lucy!" Hearing Levi call my name, I turned to

watch him walk along the path toward me, his long strides loose, relaxed. His lips turned up at the corners in a smile, which I couldn't help but return. Dacian stood, watching Levi approach.

"There you are. I got a text from Jared suggesting we meet for dinner at the café." Levi drew to a halt, looking from Dacian to me and back again.

"Good idea. Tell him yes." There was an uncomfortable silence, which Levi broke by asking, "Who's this?"

Ah yes, I'd forgotten they hadn't met yet. "This is Dacian. He's an angel."

"Really?" Levi assessed Dacian with narrowed eyes. "What sort? Arch like you?"

"Guardian," Dacian supplied, his voice clipped. Was that a hint of jealousy in his tone? *Surely not.*

"Want to join us?" Levi asked, and this time I looked at him in surprise. Did he want to spend time with Dacian?

"I do not," Dacian replied, then promptly disappeared.

"Friendly chap, isn't he?" Levi turned his attention to me, and I saw it then in his eyes, the relief that Dacian hadn't accepted the invitation. Levi had offered it to be polite, and my heart melted a little at the gesture.

"Dacian was my best friend when I was in Heaven. We lost touch after I left, and it seems he's suffered some memory loss since he doesn't remember me at all," I explained, looping my arm through Levi's and continuing my walk along the path.

"Are you and he...?" I knew what he was asking and shook my head.

"Nope. Not involved. Not anything."

"Good," he said a second before he pulled me to a halt and lowered his mouth to mine, fusing us together. He wrapped his arms around me, the hold tight, unyielding. The heat was blistering and surreal at the same time, and I felt it all the way down to my toes. He broke the kiss and nipped at my ear. "I've wanted to do that since I first laid eyes on you."

I may or may not have melted into a puddle at his feet.

***

JARED BROUGHT Nic with him to the cafe, and I wondered why since she disliked me so much. "I suggested he bring her," Levi whispered, his breath hot in my ear, making me shiver. The kiss in the park had me all distracted, and now with his thigh pressed up against mine in the booth we'd chosen, I could barely think, let alone hold a coherent conversation.

"Lucy. Levi." Jared slid into the booth opposite me, and I smiled a greeting, easing my body slightly away from Levi for some relief. I saw him look at me out of the corner of my eye, but I ignored him. If he kept this up, I wouldn't be held responsible for my actions, which would be to throw him down on the table and have my way with him, consequences be damned.

Feeling the cool stare of Nic, I focused my attention on her, giving her a small smile and nod of the head in greeting. She returned the head nod, not the smile. Awesome. Dinner was going to be fun.

"Before we order, I think we need to get something out of the way." Jared cleared his throat, and I leaned back, watching with interest. Just what did he have planned?

"Nic has made it very clear, on numerous occasions, that she doesn't believe Lucy's story. If we're to all work together—and basically get along —we need to rectify that."

A flash of annoyance appeared on Nic's face, quickly followed by her blurting out, "If you've asked me here to listen to more of her bullshit, then I'm out." She began to move as if to leave, but Jared's grasp on her wrist halted her. I saw the flush of color on her face and bit back a grin. She had it bad for him, and I sympathized. He'd yet to notice her in that way; he saw her as his work partner and nothing more.

"I don't see why we need to work with them anyway. Good old-fashioned police work will get the job done, not all this psychic medium bullshit. No offense." She aimed the last words at Levi, who shrugged, not caring what she thought.

"They can help, believe me," Jared grumbled. "My gut tells me that what we're dealing with is otherworldly. How else do you explain the autopsy results?"

"She had a heart attack, Jared. That's what the autopsy results said. There is no case; there is no dimension breach or otherworldly bullshit going on. Except this one needs a psych ward, and if she steps just one toe over the wrong side of the law, I'm going to see she enjoys the comforts of a padded cell." She pointed her finger at me, and I wasn't sure if I wanted to laugh or slap her silly.

"Lucy, can you do your thing?" Jared asked me.

"My thing?"

"The eyes."

"Oh, yeah, sure, if you want." Propping my elbows on the table, I leaned forward and settled my gaze on Nic. "Nicole James." My voice dropped as I injected a little other-world power into it, just to add to the whole ambiance of having dinner with the Devil. When her eyes met mine, I let the fires of Hell transform my usual crystal blue gaze.

"How did you do that?" she asked suspiciously, not particularly impressed. "Are they contacts?"

Jared shook his head in apparent despair, and I patted his hand. "It's okay. I've got something else that will convince her. Levi, can you let me out?"

Levi slid out of the booth, standing to one side while I slid out. I glanced around; the café was packed. This was going to burn some energy, but if it was important to Jared that Nic was in on everything, then I'd do it. With a wave of my hand, I froze the room, then turned my attention to Nic, who was watching me with a frown. I extended my wings with a flourish, not to their full extent since there wasn't enough space, but far enough that they were imposing if I do say so myself. My black feathers shone in the overhead light, and orange, red, and yellow flames danced over them in a mesmerizing display.

Nic clapped a hand over her mouth and stared, her eyes huge. I watched the color drain from her face and worried for a moment that she was about to faceplant, but she pulled herself together, sucking in a deep breath, "Oh. My. God."

"Not quite. Lucifer. At your service." I gave her a mock bow, tucked my wings away, and removed the freeze I'd placed over the café. Levi was gazing at me with what can only be described as lust in his eyes, and my knees threatened to buckle at the heat that washed through me. What was this attraction to the human? I'd had lovers in the past, but never this distracting, aching, need. The need to touch and be touched. The need to taste, to explore, to devour, for that's what I wanted, to devour him in the most erotic way.

"Lucy," Levi groaned, stepping forward, hands resting on my hips, "your eyes."

"What about them?" Bringing up my hand, I traced his jaw, feeling the soft tickle of his beard, and let my fingers trace over his lips.

"They're...I don't know; they're sort of midnight blue with stars in them?" His odd description brought me to my senses, and I stepped back, giving us some breathing room.

"What?" I blinked a couple of times, peered at Levi to see myself reflected in his eyes.

"Are you folks ready to order?" A waitress appeared, and Levi indicated I should take my seat, sliding in after me as I resumed my position in the booth. Handing me a menu, Levi quickly perused his while telling Jared and Nic to go ahead and order. It appeared Jared was the only one who had his head together at the table. Nic was gazing at me in wonder, and Levi and I were both struggling with the desire to strip each other naked. I thought I heard him groan under his breath, and by the way he adjusted himself under the table, I knew the struggle was real.

"Maybe if you stop thinking about it, that would help?" Levi leaned over to whisper in my ear. "Because I swear to God you're putting out some sort of signal that is driving me fucking wild, and while I've never been into public sex, right now I'm up for anything. *Anything.*"

His words had my imagination running wild. Not to mention the tingling in my lady parts. But he was right—we were feeding off each other. The more aroused I became, the more my energy reflected it. He was feeding off my energy and becoming more aroused himself. A cycle. Sucking in a deep breath, I closed my eyes and focused on other things. The soul stealer. How to find him. How to return him to his own realm.

It worked. I felt my energy settle, and beside me, Levi relaxed.

"Thank you," he mouthed when I glanced at him before turning my attention back to the menu.

"So you're really Lucifer," Nic said. The coolness was still in her tone, and I almost laughed aloud. Still the same Nic, full of ice.

"Correct." I nodded my head sideways, drawing her attention to the waitress who was standing at the end of the table with pen and pad in hand, waiting to take our order. Me being Lucifer wasn't a secret, but I didn't think it wise to alert the townsfolk to the soul stealer who was loose in their town.

Nic frowned but took the hint, placing her order without looking at the menu. Clearly a frequent diner. Jared followed, then Levi, and finally me. I didn't know what I ordered. I picked randomly since I was working hard to keep my focus off of sex. Even thinking about not thinking about sex was turning me on.

"Lucy!" Levi wrapped his fingers around my wrist and squeezed hard. "Cut it out."

"Sorry," I muttered, "it isn't easy. It's a two-way street, you know."

"What are you two whispering about?" Nic interrupted, and I was grateful for the distraction.

"Sex," I responded. Levi made a choking sound, Jared blushed, and Nic leaned forward with interest.

"Oh? Sex with...who? You two?"

"Time to change the subject." Levi cut in before I could answer.

"I agree." Jared backed him up, so I let it drop. I was still getting used to their human ways.

"Fine," Nic huffed, then her face lit up as an idea came to her. "So what can you do, Lucy? Are the eyes and wings it? Or do you have other powers?"

"It all depends on the situation. For example, I can do things like this." With a quick flick of my wrist, I changed her outfit from her almost staple wardrobe of worn T-shirts and baggy pants to a form-fitting little black dress. Her hair that had been hanging unstyled around her face was now a sleek and shining updo, and a light dusting of makeup transformed her dull and tired face.

"Wow." Jared breathed, his eyes traveling over Nic. "You look—amazing."

Finally! He'd finally noticed her—I hoped. Unfortunately, Nic was too distracted with her own transformation to notice him noticing her. The irony.

"H-how?" she stuttered, running her hands over the dress, then frowning. Ah, I could feel the discomfort starting to roll off her. Curious, I allowed myself to read her, not surprised by anything I discovered. I already knew Nic was a straight-laced, by-the-book cop. I also knew she had a thing for Jared that she didn't have the balls to pursue. She'd pushed her feminine side down to advance her career, to become "one of the boys." It saddened me that she felt she had to do that to succeed.

"Don't like the Audrey Hepburn look?" I got it. She wasn't a dress girl. She was a tomboy, but even a tomboy could look good. I waved my hand again, and this time she was dressed in figure-hugging black jeans, cowboy boots, and an off-the-shoulder red blouse. Her hair went from sleek updo to casual waves falling to her shoulders. Her natural makeup I left alone. She looked gorgeous. By the look on Jared's face, he agreed. Deciding I'd meddled enough, I sat back and watched the two of them.

"You look fantastic, Nic." Jared touched her hand, drawing her attention to him. "That outfit really suits you. And your hair..." Reaching up, he touched one of the curls close to her face. Her squeaked "thank you" almost had me laughing. *Awww, how cute.*

My pleasure at watching their awareness of each other unfold was interrupted by Levi suddenly gasping and leaning forward. His eyes focused on something in the distance.

"Someone's on the move," he said. I touched my hand to his and focused, channeling him. He was right: it looked like Brianna had left home. Alone.

"Where could she be going?" I asked.

Levi looked at me, shrugging a shoulder. "Probably to Sarah's house." We waited, intent on zeroing in on her location, like a mystical GPS. Only she didn't go to Sarah's house.

"The school. She's going to school? At this time of night?" I was puzzled. It was eight in the evening. Why would Brianna risk visiting the school, the one place I expressly warned her not to go to?

"Everyone's at the school tonight." Jared broke into my thoughts. "It's the Halloween party."

"Shit." Levi and I said in unison. "Do you know what this means?" Levi couldn't disguise the worry on his face.

"That's she's a sitting target for the soul stealer. Even with the bracelet, she's unprotected if he sees her." I replied.

ELEVEN

The kids had done a mighty fine job of decorating the school gym for the Halloween dance. Cardboard cut-outs of spooky trees, standing over six feet tall, each limb cut with great precision, painted in varying shades from white to black, were placed around the gym, the floor covered in a layer of smoke with lights casting different colors from green to purple. Pumpkin lights added to the effect. I was quietly impressed. This wasn't a bunch of orange and black balloons and streamers thrown around; this had to have taken months of planning and tons of hard work. I wasn't surprised Brianna wanted to attend.

I'd transported Levi and myself to the school as

soon as we'd realized that Brianna was not only at the dance but that Sarah was too, and she'd removed her talisman bracelet, leaving her a very easy target for the soul stealer. Jared and Nic were following in Jared's car, giving him time to fill her in on the way. We'd had to abandon dinner, and my stomach grumbled in protest. I'd be glad to be back in Hell where I didn't have to deal with these annoying human encumbrances.

The gym was packed with teenagers dressed as ghouls, zombies, vampires, and werewolves. Again, I was impressed with the amount of effort they'd put into their costumes. Weaving through the students, I zeroed in on the girls—at least they were together. Just as I'd get them in my sights, they'd move, and I'd lose sight of them.

"I can't track them here." Levi cursed. "Too many people. Can you see them?"

"Nah, lost sight of them. Let's split up. If you find them, get them to Jared's car and get them out of here," I told him.

"Sarah's talisman?"

"Good point. I'll go get it now." Pushing through a side door and out of sight, I extended my wings and materialized in Sarah's bedroom. Holy fuck. It looked like a bomb had gone off: clothes and shoes were strewn everywhere, and for a moment, I thought the soul stealer had found her. Then I recalled I'd just laid eyes on her myself mere minutes ago. I began searching for the talisman among the carnage that was a teenage girl's bedroom with a sigh.

Eventually, I found it under the bed. I'd be having a word with Sarah about her slovenly habits —if the soul stealer didn't get her first after this stupid stunt. Worried too much time had passed, leaving Levi alone to round up the girls, I hurried back to the dance. Levi was right. All the people, emotions, and energy running high were messing with getting a read on anyone. I couldn't even zero in on Levi to let him know I was back. I spotted Jared across the room, head and shoulders taller than everyone else. At least he'd arrived. Loud music was thumping, strobe lights flashing, and bodies gyrating. Ordinarily, I'd stop and join in the fun, for it did look like a good time just waiting to be had, but I pushed on.

"Have you found them?" Jared shouted at me, and I shook my head. Turning to Nic, he nodded his head toward the back of the gym. "We'll go check outside. They have a maze and a house of horrors setup out there."

That's when I heard it. Faint, but there. Levi, screaming my name. With no regard for anyone noticing, I flew to him, knowing my movements were so fast no one could truly be sure of what they saw. He was outside, running toward the woods that backed onto the school.

"Thank fuck," he puffed. "They're there!" He pointed as he ran, and I followed his finger to see two figures crossing the open field and into the woods. Behind them, a man. Oh shit. It was the soul stealer, had to be. I caught up with the girls with a flap of my wings, swinging in behind them, keeping my wings drawn to protect them. They were both wheezing and crying. I was trying to work out how to scoop them both up and get us out of here when I was tackled from behind.

Together we toppled, somersaulting through the brush until I came to a halt up against a tree with a resounding thud. *Ouch.* Zuska untangled himself from me and jumped to his feet, his eyes on his prey, who'd stopped and turned around to watch. Shaking my head, I rose, brushing twigs from my jeans.

"Listen up, Zuska, you don't belong here. You

need to return to your own realm." I stepped sideways, wings extended, deliberately blocking the girls from his view. He'd have to get through me to get to them.

"No can do, Satan." Gah, how did he know my brothers gave me that nickname? Did the whole fucking universe know? They were such assholes, and I knew I had to bite the bullet and deal with them once all this was over.

"Why are you even here?" I asked, watching as he shifted his weight from one foot to the other. He was getting ready to attack, of that I was sure.

"For the food. Our realm is experiencing a...what do you call it? A drought?"

"You've consumed all the souls? In your realm? Are you fucking kidding me?"

"Earth is ready to harvest. Once I am established, I will open the portal and let my brethren through. Once we are done with Earth, we will move on to the next planet, solar system, realm, whatever—it matters not where we go, for we will always find food to fuel us."

"Earth isn't yours to harvest, so I suggest you pack up your bat and ball and go along home now."

"You can't stop me." He sneered.

"Wanna bet?" I threw out a bolt of energy,

hitting him in the shoulder and sending him tumbling backward. Straightening, he eyeballed me, then threw his own power at me. Swiftly moving my wing in front of me as a shield, I deflected the blow. Glancing over my shoulder at the girls, I mouthed the word *run*. I could keep him distracted here long enough for them to get away. Still, even better, if I could contain him and bring him back to the cemetery, back to where the veil was still weak, I could get him back to his own realm.

"That all you got?" I taunted. We volleyed energy bolts at each other, and I could see he was tiring. This seemed...too easy. Then I remembered. Didn't he have a secret weapon? He'd given the glowing sword to the zombie ghosts to use against me—and it was *very* effective. I'd thought he had a more potent, more powerful weapon tucked away for his own use, so why wasn't he using it?

"Seriously, is that all you've got?" I stopped and stood, hands-on-hips, eyeing the panting soul stealer who had sweat beading on his forehead. "No weapons? Nothing?"

He shook his head, unable to speak. Well. How disappointing. It also brought to mind that if the sword *was* his, why did he give it away? So maybe the sword wasn't his at all. It wasn't him who'd given it to the zombie ghosts. Who did? Dacian? Yet he'd turned up and saved me.

My pondering cost me. Before I could stop him, Zuska dematerialized. *Fuck it all*, I cursed. I should have grabbed him instead of standing here thinking about a goddamn sword. Snapping my attention around, I zeroed in on the scream coming from the direction the girls had fled in. *Fuck*.

They were on the edge of the woods. Levi had arrived, breathless from his run across the field. All eyes were on Zuska, who had Sarah, her back pressed against his chest, his arm pulled tight across her throat.

"Stay back," he warned, eyeing us all. Brianna was silently crying, tears streaming down her cheeks, and Sarah was clawing at the soul stealer's arms, trying to ease the crushing grip he had on her neck, gasping for breath.

"Let her go," I demanded.

"No chance."

He'd already slipped past me once. I couldn't let it happen again. I glanced at Levi, who was looking from me to Zuska and back again. I needed Zuska to turn to the left, just slightly. That would give me a clear shot. A single bolt of energy to the head. It might not kill him, but I was hoping it would be enough for him to loosen his grip on Sarah, and I could snatch her from him, or better yet, capture him. My eyes met Levi's, and I gave the slightest of nods. He nodded in return. Yes, he understood.

With a bellow, Levi launched forward. A split second later, I followed, my hand extended, reaching for Sarah's wrist. As soon as Levi had yelled, she'd extended her arm as if reaching for him. For help. I was within reach, my fingers wrapped around her wrist. I tugged, and she stumbled toward me. It had worked—Zuska had loosened his hold on her with the sudden attack from Levi.

Levi stormed forward, wrapping his arms around Zuska's waist and driving them backward. Pushing Sarah toward Brianna, I turned my attention to the fighting pair, who were now on the ground. Levi had Zuska on his back, straddling his waist when Zuska smacked him in the head with something in his hand—a rock. Levi groaned and toppled sideways, and soon their positions were reversed. This wasn't good, not good at all. I watched in horror as Zuska opened his mouth wide and began to lower his face to Levi's. He was going to eat his soul!

"Get away from him, asshole." Red light shot

from my fingers, knocking Zuska off Levi. Reaching down, I tried to drag Levi to his feet. Still groggy from the blow to his head, Levi tried, but his feet wouldn't obey, he was dragging me down, and I couldn't get a decent grip on him. The distraction with Levi was all the soul stealer needed. Suddenly he was no longer in front of me. He was behind us, and he had Sarah in his arms, his mouth open over hers, sucking her soul from her body. I threw an energy bolt at him, but he shifted, using her body as a shield, and in a matter of seconds, he was done, and she was gone. His body suffused with color, then settled, and I realized he'd taken on more of a human appearance than before. When he smiled, the pointy teeth were gone, replaced by a straight row of pearly whites.

"You're next." He grinned at Brianna and then dematerialized, letting Sarah's lifeless body fall to the ground with a thud.

Brianna fell to her knees beside her friend, crying hysterically. Anger rolled through me, and I felt it building. Anger that he'd gotten to this realm in the first place, anger that I hadn't been able to stop him, anger that another soul had been taken. It poured through me like molten lava, burning my nerve endings, increasing my heart rate, heating my skin until I thought I'd burst from it. Instead, I tipped my head back and roared. The sound echoed overhead, booming like thunder, the sound an eerie warning—the Devil was riled, and you'd better get out of her way.

TWELVE

"Now what?" Levi groaned, still on his knees, holding a hand to his bleeding head.

I fought so many things at once. Pain, agony, helplessness, and anger. The anger was all mine. I clenched my jaw so tight, my teeth hurt. I dragged in a breath, trying to calm myself. Overhead, clouds gathered, rolling and tumbling blacker than the night, with flashes of red lightning streaking through them. This was what happened when I lost my temper when I lost control. Thunder cracked again, loud and vicious, and Brianna flinched, peering up at me with terrified eyes. I felt her pain as if it were a physical thing, mixing with my anger and thundering through my veins until my body vibrated with it.

This had to end. I'd been pussyfooting around too long, trying to keep the balance between right and wrong, good and evil, and it had cost an innocent her life.

"I should have killed him," I cursed, turning my back on them and looking at the horizon, sucking in calming breaths, pushing away the clouds and storm rolling overhead.

"Why didn't you?" Levi asked.

"I'm not here to extinguish life." I shrugged. I'd always had a very definitive idea of what the right thing to do was, the right course of action, and it had held me in good stead. That was why I'd been given Hell. Because I would do the right thing, the fair thing. But since being topside, everything had gone pear-shaped. I'd been injured by the sword because I refused to banish the ghosts, wanting to allow them to cross over via a reaper. Mistake number one. Then I'd been trying to return the soul stealer to his own realm rather than destroy him. Mistake number two. I couldn't afford any more mistakes.

"Call Jared. Tell him where we are. He needs to deal with Sarah."

Turning my attention to Brianna, I placed a hand on her shoulder and poured some of my essence into her, calming her, soothing the pain. I wouldn't take it away altogether; that wasn't fair, neither to Brianna or Sarah, but I could help.

"Take my hand," I told her. She did, and I transported her to her front door, waiting until she'd let herself in before returning to the field. Levi was still on the ground, and it wasn't until I took a good look at him that I noticed the sheer volume of blood that continued to trickle through his fingers that were pressed to his temple. Mistake number three.

Kneeling by his side, I pulled his hand away, placed my own against his wound, and healed him. "I'm sorry."

"For what?" He sounded genuinely puzzled.

"For all of this. This was my fault. I made the wrong decision, tried to spare the soul stealer's life, and you were injured, and Sarah killed. It could have been avoided."

"You did what you thought was right." I didn't know why he was arguing with me, but the more I thought about it, the more my anger increased, and the storm that I'd sent on its way began to return; this time, the clouds tinged with red.

"What's going on, Lucy?" Levi grasped my extended hand and pulled himself to his feet.

"I'm pissed off. The weather is reflecting that. I need to get myself under control."

Once upright, Levi staggered, and I caught him. "Whoa. You okay?"

"Dizzy," he groaned, putting a hand to his head again. Shit. I hoped it was the after-effects of being healed and not something more sinister.

"Lean on me. I'll fill Jared and Nic in on what happened and then get you home. You just need to sleep it off." I hoped.

Levi dropped my hand and shook his head. "I'll sit."

The stubborn male would rather sit on the ground than lean against me. I pushed down the twinge of hurt at his rejection. He'd just been smacked in the head, hard, with a rock. While I'd healed him, the process itself often drained the victims of energy, leaving them woozy and disorientated. Rest was the answer, and if he wanted to sit in the dirt, so be it.

Jared and Nic were running across the field toward us, and while I waited, I crouched by Sarah's side. Placing a hand on her shoulder, I examined what the soul stealer had done. Just like Emily, her soul was ripped out of her. Only the tattered edges remained. Feeling along the edges, I soaked up every last trace of him. If I could get enough of his essence, I just might be able to track him.

"Fuck." Nic cursed, kneeling and checking Sarah's pulse.

"This isn't good." Jared shook his head, pulled out his phone, and dialed.

"What happened? Is he okay?" Nic stood, hands-on-hips, glanced at Levi, then back at me.

"He was hurt, but he'll be okay. I'll take him home in a moment. The soul stealer got her."

"So the almighty Lucifer wasn't good enough to stop him?" Her lip curled up in a sneer, and I wanted to wipe it off her face with my fist. The only thing that stopped me was the fact that she was right. I'd been so convinced I could easily take care of this, get the creature back to his own realm, yet here we were, another dead girl at my feet. I'd failed. It didn't sit well with me. Not at all.

I didn't respond. What could I say? Nothing. I had nothing in defense of what had occurred here tonight. Jared finished on the phone and looked at me.

"You okay?"

"I'm pissed." I kept my voice even, but I could

hear the steely undertone, the distant rumble of thunder I was barely keeping under control.

"You're the cause of the storm clouds? The thunder?"

"I lost my temper." I shrugged. Why were we talking about such inane things? "I've got to get Levi home. The soul stealer hit him in the head, and while I've healed him, he's going to need to rest. How are you going to spin this?" I indicated Sarah's body.

"Possibly drug-related." Jared shrugged. "Two young girls, dead of unknown causes, we can most likely attribute to some new party drug on the scene that is so far undetectable in the blood."

I nodded, hating that we were tarnishing the girl's reputation. This had all gone horribly wrong, and it was my fault. Another boom of thunder, and Jared winced.

"Go. I've called the ME's office. We'll take it from here."

WHILE LEVI SLEPT, I Googled. All night long, I searched, jotted down notes, perused the never-ending feed of posts on social media. I didn't understand why humans preferred to communicate this way but shrugged. If it would give me clues on where Zuska was holed up, I'd use it. Someone, somewhere, would have seen something, noticed something—and probably posted it on the internet.

Google was pretty darn good, I had to admit. I'd managed to get my hands on tons of blueprints of old city buildings, photographs of how Shadow Falls looked a hundred years ago, not only the official history of the city but anecdotes as well. Not all of it was useful, but I kept at it. Digging my hand into the bowl of candy by my side, I shoved a handful into my mouth, chewing. The sugar rush kept me sustained.

"Morning." Levi appeared in the bedroom doorway, his hair mussed, his lids hooded with the thick remnants of sleep, wearing nothing but a pair of track pants. I drank in the sight of his bare flesh, the clearly defined abs, the dusting of hair over his chest that led into a thicker trail running down and disappearing beneath the waistband of his track pants. With a curse, I scooped more candy into my mouth and turned my attention to the laptop. That was another thing I'd decided while he'd slept. No more touching, kissing, or fantasizing about Levi. From now on, he was off-limits.

"How are you feeling?" I asked, not taking my eyes off the screen but watching him from my peripheral vision anyway. So weak, I chided myself.

"Good. Better. What are you doing?" He sauntered over, running his fingers through his hair, and I quickly put my hand up to my chin to make sure I wasn't drooling.

"Research." I blew out a breath of relief when he continued on to the kitchen after a quick glance over my shoulder.

"On?"

"Shadow Falls. The soul stealer is hiding out here somewhere. I'm going to find him."

"Right." I could hear him moving about in the kitchen but resolutely kept my eyes on the laptop screen. Up until he said those three little words that every girl longs to hear. When they slipped from his mouth with effortless ease, I practically sprained my neck I swiveled it so fast to look at him.

With one corner of his mouth tipping sensually, he asked, "Want some coffee?"

And I fell. I fell hard. My determination to keep him at arm's length evaporated like mist on a hot summer's day.

"I think you're out," I finally admitted.

"What? How much did you drink?" He finally noticed the scattered coffee mugs around me.

"What?" I asked in all innocence. So I'd had a few cups of coffee, so what?

"Lucy…" He studied my face intently. "How long is it since you've slept?"

"I don't need sleep!"

"Yeah. You do. You told me yourself that the atmosphere here on Earth affects you differently. That you need to eat and sleep more frequently than what you would in Hell." Leaving the kitchen and the coffee he'd intended to prepare, he came to stand in front of me.

"Pft. I can push through. This is more important than sleep." I waved my hand at the laptop, almost sending it toppling off my lap. I quickly righted it.

"And the candy? You're using it to keep yourself awake." His voice was accusing, and I frowned. What was so wrong with wanting to stay awake? I was ready to argue with him when what he did next had my words frozen in my throat.

"Sweetheart"—cupping my face in his hands, he crouched so we were eye to eye— "you need to rest. You'll be better equipped to fight the soul stealer if you're fully rested." Damn him, he had a point, and if he called me sweetheart again, I'd do anything he wanted. Anything. Pesky human.

I blinked, a long, slow blink, for once at a loss for words. He smiled, dropped a kiss on my nose, then whispered, his lips inches from mine, "How about a quick nap? For me?"

Was he playing me? Oh, the cheeky bastard. Two could play at this game. Rather than answer, I closed the gap between our mouths, my lips settling against his, and the simmering heat that was always there went up in flames.

"Lucy." He pulled away, his deep, sexy voice all deep and, well, sexy. "You're playing with fire."

My gaze lifted from his chest to his face. "My favorite thing."

He chuckled, and I was lost. I leaped into his arms, literally, and pressed my mouth to his. He returned my kiss enthusiastically, pulling me close as his tongue sought mine, his hand entwined in my hair. Pulling back slightly, he outlined my lips with his tongue, gently drawing my bottom lip into his mouth, his teeth grazing my lip as he slowly released it. Trailing his tongue agonizingly slowly down to my jaw and then to the hollow of my throat, the jolt of ecstasy overwhelming. Tugging his hair, I pulled his head back up. His mouth met mine in a hot, desperate kiss, and I wrapped my arms around his neck.

At some point, before we landed on the sofa, I conjured our clothes away, leaving us naked in each other's arms. Our bodies seemed to fit together perfectly as if we were made for each other. Levi's fingertips trailed gently across my bare skin, leaving shudders of pleasure in their wake. His warm mouth nibbled my earlobe, gently sucking and biting at my neck. I caressed his back, luxuriating in the heat emanating from his body, the hardness of his muscles, the way he smelt and tasted. I had never wanted someone so much.

THIRTEEN

I slept for two hours. When I awoke, I was still on the sofa, tucked beneath a blanket. Levi was no longer by my side, but I sensed him in the building and guessed he was downstairs in his shop, most likely working since I could feel another energy signature.

Swinging my legs off the sofa, I bit back the gasp of surprise when Levi's grandmother appeared before me.

"Hello." I remained seated and waited. She was here to give me a message, of that I was sure. To warn me to leave her grandson alone, no doubt.

"Relax." She half-smiled before her face became serious again. "Levi is a good man."

"He's very good." I nodded.

"But he is not why I'm here."

"He's not?" I was surprised. I was sure she was here to give me a serve for fooling around with her grandson.

"This otherworld creature you seek…"

"The soul stealer? You know where he is?" Why hadn't I thought to ask the spirit world?

"Not exactly. You need to look lower."

"Look lower? What do you mean?"

"And you might want to think about putting some clothes on." She disappeared, and I glanced down. I'd forgotten I was naked. Nice. Having a good old chat with Grandma in the nude. Levi would be impressed. I pondered what she'd told me while conjuring up another set of designer jeans, shirt, and jacket. *Look lower*. What did that mean? I looked at my feet. Lower. Downstairs? Was the answer in Levi's shop?

Hurrying downstairs, I waited while Levi finished up the reading with a middle-aged woman. He walked her to the door, then turned, and the smile he laid on me had me weak at the knees. It was filled with…sin. His smile promised all that we'd done earlier and more. Flicking the sign on the door to closed and locking it, he walked to me, his stride full of purpose. Again I had to hope I wasn't drooling because this guy was so hot, so goddamn stunning it was as if he'd been created for me alone.

He stopped, standing so close his chest brushed mine, and I couldn't stop myself from thrusting my chest out for closer contact. We eyed each other, breath mingling, then I was propelled backward so fast my back hit the wall with a thud. The pictures hanging on it rattled and hung off balance. Neither of us cared. Pinning my wrists beside my head, he plundered my mouth, his tongue dueling with mine. I let my energy wash over him, let it explore the hills and valleys of his muscles as they contracted and released under my touch. "How are you doing that?" he growled, knowing my wrists were pinned, that I wasn't touching him with my hands.

"My essence," I breathed. "Try it." I felt the tentative brush of his energy against the nape of my neck, slowly drifting down, over my shoulder, to my breast, hotter than his touch, burning, searing my flesh away. The groan that left my mouth was wanton, to say the least.

I returned my attention back to my own exploration, felt the smoothness of his skin, the hardness of the muscles underneath, the tautness of his abdomen. Suddenly a flash of something caught my eye. I focused on the figure behind Levi's shoulder.

"Your grandmother!" I gasped.

Lifting his head, he looked at me, puzzled. "My grandmother?" She winked at me and disappeared. I was trembling, my body still burning from the fire Levi had started but hadn't put out. Damn it.

"Yes." Pushing against his chest, I forced him to take a step back, to give me a reprieve from the heat seeping into me from his nearness.

"What about her?"

"She visited me. Upstairs."

"She did?" Surprise colored his voice.

I nodded. "She had a message."

"For me? Why didn't she come to me?" His surprise turned to hurt, and just like that, any remaining desire was doused like a bucket of ice water tipped over my head.

"Babe, she's been with you this whole time," I reassured him. "She kept herself hidden from you because you were hurting. Grieving. I'm sure she'll reveal herself to you soon."

"What?"

Realizing I'd let the proverbial cat out of the bag, I explained, "She came with you when you moved here and has been watching over you this entire time. She loves you as much as you love her."

"I didn't know. Didn't feel her at all."

"Because she didn't want you to. Look, I'll let you hash it out with her later, but for now—"

"Wait," he cut in, "is she here now?"

"No. Listen to me. Upstairs, when I woke up, she appeared in front of me and told me to look lower. Do you know what that means?"

"Look lower? No, I don't."

Damn it, I'd been hoping he would understand the meaning. We both glanced at the floor. How low were we talking?

"It's about the soul stealer? She knows about him?"

"She said she hasn't actually seen him, so can't give us an exact location, and maybe what she does know of him she's learned from us, I don't really know, but with her psychic abilities, maybe she's feeling his energy too, and because she's a spirit she can follow it better than we can."

"Ask her!" he demanded, and I looked at him.

"She's not here, Levi. I told you, I don't lie."

"But you didn't tell me she was here," he accused.

"She asked me not to. When I first saw her, I was

going to tell you—she didn't want that. I honored her wishes."

He continued to stare at me as if assessing if I was telling the truth or not. I could see the hurt in his aura as well as his expression, but there was also a hint of anger as well. At me. I sighed. I seemed to be getting everything wrong this trip topside. Ignoring me, he stalked to the door and flipped the sign back around and unlocked the door.

"I've got work to do." His meaning was clear. Leave him alone. Fine. If it was space he wanted, it was space he'd get.

Retreating back upstairs, I resumed my position on the sofa with his laptop, candy, and replenished coffee. I was perusing the Shadow Falls Historical Society webpage, reading about the tunnels running beneath what was now the town square, when it hit me. *Lower*. Underground! Look underground.

Fingers flying over the keyboard, I examined the original plans for the buildings surrounding the square. One of them, if not all, would have access to the tunnels, and my gut was telling me the soul stealer was hiding in the tunnels. How far did they go? There was no map detailing the tunnels themselves, but I found one of the town hall that showed a staircase leading below ground—and there was no cellar or basement in the town hall, which was unusual in itself. Pulling up the most recent blueprints, I searched for where the staircase would be now. My best guess: the kitchen at the rear of the hall.

I debated going downstairs and telling Levi but decided against it. I knew he was trying to summon his grandmother from the energy I could feel swirling around down there—they clearly needed to talk. Maybe then he'd quit being angry at me. Releasing my wings, I materialized in the parking lot behind the town hall. For what was to come, it was best if no one saw me. I had a soul stealer to take care of.

CHAPTER

FOURTEEN

The back of the town hall was locked, but the key I conjured took care of it, the glowing red skeleton key sliding perfectly into the keyhole with a satisfying click as it did its job. Stepping inside, I quietly closed the door and listened. No one else was here, which was a good thing. I knew from my research that the hall was used for community events, that dance classes and sometimes scout meetings were held here, but for now, it was empty.

The back door opened directly into the massive kitchen, decked out to cater for hundreds. However, the ovens and other appliances looked dated. Across the room were several cupboards, and I crossed to them. Inside one of these cupboards was the entrance to the tunnels; I was sure of it. The first door I opened revealed shelves, all stacked with white crockery. The next door was similar, only this one held what appeared to be tablecloths. The third door was a walk-in pantry. Bingo. Stepping inside, I pulled the string dangling from the light bulb hanging from the ceiling, and the small room was bathed in yellow light. Shelves ran around the entire room. Closing my eyes, I visualized the original floor plan. There. I turned to the back of the pantry. Behind that wall should be the staircase. If the soul stealer was down there, this hadn't been his point of entry. But it was mine.

With a silent apology, I demolished the shelves and ripped out the wall, tossing the debris to the floor and stepping over it. Sure enough, an empty cavity behind the wall, and a stone staircase, leading down. Summoning a ball of light, I balanced it in my palm and began to make my way down the stairs. The air was stale and cool, getting colder the lower I went. For some reason, I'd imagined the walls to be damp and covered in moss or lichen, but it was the opposite. Dry. Dusty. Crumbling.

At the bottom of the staircase, another room. This one held old torch sconces on the wall. There was a barrel, falling apart, sitting off to one side, and thick dust on the floor. To the left, what looked like a barn door, only smaller. Grasping the handle, I turned. Locked. With another conjured key, the door unlocked with a groaning protest, the mechanism seized with lack of use. Pushing open the door, I peered inside. A tunnel. Long and straight, and from where I stood, never-ending.

"Here goes nothing."

The tunnels were a labyrinth. At the end of the first one, it opened up into a round room, with four other tunnels branching off. I examined the floor, which was no longer a floor but simply dirt and rock beneath my feet. No sign of footprints. No one had been this way. Choosing the tunnel to my immediate left, I set off, keeping my pace slow, sending out my senses, searching for the energy signature of the soul stealer. I'd expected it to be stronger down here, for I was convinced he was here somewhere, yet the constant hum that was him was no different.

Three hours later and I was incredibly lost. The tunnels went for miles and miles. Every now and then, I'd come across a big room which housed makeshift cots, a half dozen chairs, tables. Wooden crates and a couple of barrels sat against the walls. What had they used these rooms for? To hide, obviously, but from what? What threat was so great they hid miles under the earth, in a rabbit warren of tunnels?

I was considering turning back when I felt an agitation from Levi through our bond. He'd been quiet until now, and I guessed he'd gone upstairs to look for me and discovered me missing. Not wanting to cause him undue distress, I'd just extended my wings, preparing to leave, when I heard it. A muffled cry. Someone was down here. Was it the soul stealer? I was torn. Return to Levi or search for the owner of that cry. Although it was a close call, the latter won out as the urge to return to Levi, to continue my exploration of him, to feed my starved desire for him was all-consuming.

Rather than leave the tunnels, I propelled my way forward, using speed now, darting up and down, round and round until I came into a clearing and stopped in surprise. There, chained to the wall, was Dacian.

"Dacian?" I glanced around, checking to see if anyone else was there. The chamber was empty, except for Dacian, suspended with arms outstretched, his toes barely touching the ground, tape over his mouth. Who had done this? Who could restrain an angel?

I instructed the ball of light I was carrying to levitate, freeing my hands. Dacian was shaking his head at me and making noises as I reached for his chains, only to snatch my hand away at the painful jolt as soon as I made contact with the metal. What the Hell?

"What's going on? Who did this?" Reaching up, I ripped the tape from his mouth, and he winced.

"It's a trap!" he shouted. I spun, hands raised, ready to blast anyone who attacked. Only...no one did. There was no one else here, just Dacian and me.

"Are you sure?" I asked, peering around, holding my stance in front of him.

"Yes."

"By who?"

"The soul stealer."

"Where is he then?"

"He's here." Dacian seemed sure. Could I trust him? I didn't know, but I couldn't work out why he would lie. If he meant me harm, he wouldn't have warned me it was a trap. I shrugged. It was a lousy trap if that were the case.

I waited, crouching slightly in front of Dacian, ready to do battle. Only no one attacked.

"Are you really sure?" I asked.

"I'm really sure." He was angry, but underneath

the anger was concern. For me? Or for his own sorry ass? Straightening up, I kept my back to him while surveying the room. Seconds ticked by, which turned into minutes. Eventually, I lowered my arms and turned to Dacian.

"We're alone. Let's get you down."

"He's here. It's a trap. I know it is," Dacian argued.

"Fine. It may well be a trap, but it hasn't sprung yet." I touched the chains holding Dacian to the wall, and again a painful jolt shot through me. "What the Hell are these made from?" I asked him. "Do they hurt?"

"They're burning like a motherfucker," he gritted. "Don't know what they're made from, but it's not from this realm."

Blowing out a breath, I brought my hands up in front of me and began drawing red symbols in the air. One of them would work to release the chains; I just had to find which one. With each failure, I'd swipe it away, the red lines breaking apart and falling to the ground like ash.

"Finally." Dacian dropped to the ground once I'd found the correct key to unlock him.

"You're welcome." I couldn't stop the sarcasm,

but he ignored me, busy healing his bloodied wrists where the chains had burned him.

"How long have you been here?" I turned my back and swept the room again. Nothing had changed. No enemy had launched at us. I wondered if he was delirious if whatever was in those chains was toxic.

"A day or two. I'm not sure. It was so dark I couldn't tell if it was night or day, couldn't measure the passing of time."

"How did he capture you?" I was curious and a little weary. Dacian had made it clear in the past that he didn't trust me. How did I know this wasn't some elaborate setup? Although, I couldn't see him sacrificing himself by playing the victim to lay a trap for me. That was not Dacian's style.

Before he could answer, the room began to shake. It started as a soft tremor, then built in intensity. Dust and small pebbles fell from the walls and ceiling, then a bigger rock fell, followed by another.

"We need to get out of here!" Dacian yelled, extending his wings, ready for flight.

"This way!" We flew from the room, rocks falling around us, and then the weirdest thing. The walls began turning, clicking, and sliding together like cogs in a machine. The tip of my wing got caught in between the moving walls, crushing the end.

"Ouch!" I snatched my wings in, soothing the sting and healing myself as I did so. "No more flying, put your wings away," I yelled at Dacian, glancing over my shoulder to see him do exactly that. With the moving tunnels and crushing rocks, our wings were no longer available to us. We'd have to go old school and run.

It didn't help that I was hopelessly lost before we'd begun our mad dash. Now everything was moving, twisting, turning. What once was the floor was now the wall, and then the ceiling. I ran into an open cavern only to have the floor split in half, one side going up, the other going down, and endless gaping darkness in the void in between.

"Jump!" Dacian yelled from behind me. I did, grabbing hold of the edge of the floor that was level with my head and scrambling up, quickly turning to extend my hand to Dacian. He jumped, missed the rock, but I caught him around the wrist. The weight of him almost pulled me off the edge, and I grunted, scrambling with my free hand to wedge my fingers into the rocks to hold on and not slide off.

Dacian dangled. He looked up at me, and I saw the determination in his eyes. He quickly glanced around and then used his wings to boost himself up and onto the moving floor. He sat next to me, panting.

"Thanks for that."

"Anytime, but just for the record, what the fuck is going on? What's all this?" Our platform was traveling up and up, the rocks above our heads moving out of the way. Then it stopped, twisted, and began to tilt. We slid off onto a smaller platform below and started the same crazy journey over and over again.

Running, jumping, dodging. We were both panting and winded, and I feared no closer to finding a way out. It was like a moving maze with no respite. Was this the doing of the soul stealer? But he'd seemed relatively weak on my encounters with him, not capable of this amount of magic. I hated that he had me second-guessing myself and that, in turn, notched up my anger levels, and I thought I heard a boom of thunder overhead.

"Was that you?" Dacian asked, running by my side. We were both scraped and bloody, with no time for healing.

"I think so." Which could only mean one thing. We had to be close to the surface. "Stay close," I told him. I focused on my anger, let it grow and build. I played over in my mind the death of Sarah, Levi getting hurt, the soul stealer getting away, then I thought of my brothers and the unfair way they treated me. The thunder was louder now, and rather than tamping it down, I let it grow. I could feel it within me, like lava in my veins, knew my eyes would be flames, caught glimpses of red forks of lightning sparking from my fingertips.

I reached for Dacian with one hand, clamping my fingers around his wrist, and with the other hand, I shot a blast of lightning into the rocks above us. It coincided with a massive boom from overhead. The rocks moving in their strange formation shattered, and we were falling. Shielding my face with my free arm, I spread my wings and propelled us up through the rocks, dirt, dust, and debris, Dacian still clutched tight. He was a dead weight until he used his own wings to boost us up.

We burst through into fresh air. I flew us clear of the massive hole that had opened in the earth. Setting us down, I collapsed onto my back, panting, looking at the angry red clouds overhead that were now receding.

"You okay?" I turned my head, looking at Dacian, who was splayed by my side, strangely quiet.

"You saved me." He turned his head to meet my eyes.

"Of course I did, you idiot."

"Why would you do that?"

"Because we're friends. Duh." I could hear sirens in the distance. The humans were coming.

"After all I've done? After the things I said?"

I sat up, wrapping my arms around my knees. "That's what friendship is." I shrugged. "To me anyway."

"Lucy!" Levi was shouting, and I looked up to see him running toward me, his face a mask of panic and concern. I then became aware of our surroundings. I'd blown a hole in the town square, right in the middle of the park.

Skidding to his knees by my side, he clasped my head in his hands and peered at me intently, his eyes running all over me. "Are you okay? Are you hurt?" His thumb brushed against the edge of a scrape on my cheek, and I felt the sting.

"I'm fine." I smiled, healing myself of all the scrapes and bruises.

"What. The. Fuck. Happened?" He pulled me to my feet and dragged me further back from the edge of the hole.

"I'm not entirely sure," I admitted. I told him

how I'd found Dacian, how Dacian had thought the whole thing was a trap, which in hindsight, it most likely was. But there was a lot of magic involved in the trap. I wasn't sure I could lay this one at the soul stealer's door.

A fire engine pulled up, followed by an ambulance and police car. Soon the park was swarming with emergency services personnel. Dacian disappeared without a word.

"Are you hurt?" Jared appeared by my side, his badge clipped to his belt. He was here in an official capacity.

"I'm fine. Just a little grubby." I indicated my torn and dusty clothes.

"What happened? Did you see?" His eyes bored into mine, and I almost laughed. He was trying to send me a message—*don't reveal the truth to the people milling around us*. I winked to reassure him I wasn't an absolute idiot.

"Sort of. It happened so fast. I was running. This storm rolled in real quick when there was a massive clap of thunder, and suddenly this sinkhole just appeared. The earth fell away beneath my feet, but I managed to pull myself out." It was plausible. Sort of. And technically not a lie.

"Was anyone else here? Is anyone in the sinkhole?"

I shook my head. "No." I knew Jared wasn't asking about supernatural beings. He was worried innocent humans had disappeared down what appeared to be a bottomless hole. I leaned closer so the others couldn't hear. "FYI, there is a massive labyrinth of tunnels down there. You could maybe look into that at some point."

"Tunnels?" he repeated.

"Old. Ancient. Maybe built by the settlers of Shadow Falls." I shrugged. I didn't know why they were there, just that they were.

"You should let the medics check you out." Jared straightened, nodding.

"I'm fine." In fact, I felt pretty good. Releasing my anger the way I did left me feeling cleansed and calm. "But a shower is in order. I'll be at Levi's if you need me."

Levi slid his fingers between mine, our palms pressed together, and hand in hand, we walked back to his apartment. I was glad he was no longer angry at me. I needed his help to solve the ever-deepening puzzle of what the fuck was going on in Shadow Falls.

FIFTEEN

"I'm sorry," Levi whispered against my neck, and I shivered. Warm water poured over us, making our skin slick. It was my first shower with a human, and I could easily become addicted to sharing a shower with one Levi Forrester.

"You're forgiven." I gasped in response, not really focusing on his words but the nip of his teeth and soothing motion of his tongue. I knew he was apologizing for being angry with me over his grandmother, and I loved that he'd done so, but man, that mouth of his. As if sensing I wasn't paying attention, he lifted his head and cupped my face in his hands.

"I didn't mean to take it out on you." His words

were solemn and his face serious. Leaning forward, I placed my mouth on his, halting his words. We were naked in his shower. The last thing I wanted to be talking about, let alone thinking about, was his grandmother.

"You're forgiven."

He grinned and reached behind me for the loofah, squeezing a liberal amount of shower gel on it before pulling back, his hooded eyes full of promise.

"Let's get you clean."

The brush of the loofah over my sensitive skin raised goosebumps over my flesh wherever it traced. I reached for him, wanting the torture to be over, but he tutted me and pushed my hands away. "I'm not done yet." After spending what felt like eternity thoroughly cleaning the front of my body, from my collarbone to my toes and everything in between, he twirled his finger in the air, indicating I should turn. I wasn't sure my legs would cooperate. I'd locked them into position to keep myself upright during his sensual assault—now he wanted me to turn. Figuring he'd catch me if I face-planted, I obeyed, slowly turning to face the tile, placing my hands on it for balance.

When his hands settled on my shoulders and

began to massage, my head fell forward, and my forehead met the tile with an audible *thunk*. His hands were magic. They soothed tense muscles I didn't know were tense, yet at the same time, they burned a path right to my core. He nudged one of my feet with his. "Spread 'em," he growled. I did. "Wider." I shook with desire, eager for what was to come. His hands ran down my sides, over my hips, resting on my thighs. My whole body ached for him, his touch arousing sensations and feelings I had never experienced before.

"You have the most amazing body Lucy" his voice growled huskily in my ear. "I don't know what you are doing to me, but I've never wanted anybody the way I want you."

With the combination of the hot water caressing my body, the increased sensations from being covered in shower gel, Levi's sheer masculinity, I was transported to a place of pleasure I had never before experienced, and I abandoned myself to it entirely.

***

"Tell me what really happened today—and why there's a massive hole in the middle of the town square." Levi had surprised me by holding off on the questions, but now, both of us clean and sated, he wanted to know. And I didn't blame him. Stretched out on the sofa, my head in his lap, I quickly filled him in on what had happened, leaving nothing out.

With his fingers idly running up and down my arm, it was getting harder and harder to concentrate. Thankfully Levi cut in. "So you're saying something—maybe the soul stealer—captured Dacian. Held him captive with mystical chains. In the tunnels no one knew existed under our town."

"Pretty much," I agreed.

"But you're not convinced the soul stealer is responsible?"

I shook my head. "It makes no sense. If the soul stealer had such power, why would he capture Dacian? Why not kill him? As far as I know, the soul stealer doesn't even know about Dacian. He was never with us in any of our confrontations with the soul stealer. So why take him? And then hide him down there? For what purpose?"

"Dacian said it was a trap...for you? Did whoever set this up know you'd go looking for Dacian?"

"But I didn't! I didn't even know he was missing. And I should have. He's been pretty much following me around since I got here. Keeping his distance, but I knew he was there, watching. But now that I think about it, I hadn't seen him for a couple of days, but I just didn't notice." And for that, I felt terrible.

Mr. Meow jumped up onto my stomach, meowing for attention. I ran my fingers through his soft fur.

"Who else then? Your brothers?" I'd filled Levi in on the history with Gabriel and Michael. Was it them? Another prank? But those days were gone, surely. We were no longer newly created angels in Heaven, fooling around and having fun as we learned our craft and trained for our roles. This was too extreme for a prank, even for them. Dacian had been hurt by the chains.

Blowing out a frustrated breath, I closed my eyes. "I don't know. I really have no idea what's going on." It drove me crazy to admit it. The soft rumble of Mr. Meow's purr vibrating through me lulled me, and I drifted, dozing as my mind tried to make sense of today's events.

"Well, isn't this a Hallmark card moment," a voice drawled. Mr. Meow hissed, digging his claws into my stomach as he launched himself over the back of the sofa, his paws skidding on the floor as he fled from the room.

"What do you want, Dacian?" Levi had stiffened beneath me at the sudden appearance of the angel. With a resigned sigh, I sat up, brushing my hair back over my shoulder.

"Have you told him yet?" Dacian nodded his head at Levi, who frowned in response.

"Told me what?"

"Don't be an asshole," I scolded, frowning at Dacian. There was something different about him. He'd been slowly thawing toward me, but now I could see the cold hatred was back. What was going on with him?

"You know you two can never truly be together, right?" Ignoring me, Dacian plowed ahead. "That you don't have a future. All this fucking is just that. Sex. Nothing more."

"What we're doing is none of your goddamn business." Levi stood, and I recognized that stance. Shoulders back, feet apart. He was getting ready to take a swing, and I didn't blame him. Dacian was being a jerk. Only what he'd said? The part about not having a future? That was true; the reality was... there was no future for Levi and me. And the pain that quickly followed that truth lanced through me. I didn't want it to end, what I had with Levi; it felt so right, but...I'm Lucifer, CEO of Hell. And he was human. A good, decent human who, when his time was up on Earth, would be going to Heaven. A place I hadn't visited since I left a million lifetimes ago. There was no happy ever after for us, and the thought made my heartache.

Levi entwined my fingers with his, holding my hand tight. His eyes met mine, and I knew he saw the sadness reflected there, for he tugged me closer until we were chest to chest and kissed me. When he started to pull away from the kiss, I grabbed his head and held on, plundering his mouth with my tongue, pushing all my desire, want, lust into that kiss. My own passion rose in response, and it was like it had always been with us. Electric.

"Yeah, okay, you two, message received. You're hot for each other. You've got the chemistry. Too bad it's not enough." Dacian's tone was gloating, and I did the one thing I thought I'd never do. I zapped him. A spark of red lightning hit him in the chest and sent him somersaulting backward. I was so sick of him being an asshole, of toying with my feelings, letting me think we had something to salvage from our friendship only to turn around and try to hurt me all over again.

"Get out," I growled, releasing Levi and facing Dacian, who was brushing himself off and looking at me with a smirk. *Asshole.* He disappeared without comment, and the apartment was silent in his wake.

"What did he mean?" I knew Levi would ask, had prayed he wouldn't, but I knew it was coming. I was selfish, hoping I could stay in my—our—bubble just a little longer.

"Ignore him. He's a jerk." Stepping to the window, I gazed out, watching the activity in the town square. The area had been taped off. People were taking selfies with the hole in the background.

"Are you using me?" His words were flat, and I glanced over my shoulder at him. He was still standing in front of the sofa, arms by his sides, hands clenched into fists. Poor Levi.

"No," I whispered. "I'm not." It was all the reassurance I could give him, but it seemed that was all he needed, for he visibly relaxed.

"You've gotten under my skin, Lucy," he told me, striding across the room, steps confident and sure. My heart melted. As did my panties. Levi in alpha mode was hot.

"Ditto," was my witty response. The fire burning in his eyes made my stomach flutter, and it crossed my mind that Levi was not only under my skin, but he was also working his way into my heart.

SIXTEEN

"Are you sure it's safe?" Levi asked for the millionth time.

"I'm reasonably sure. And if it isn't, I'll get you out. I promise." I knew he was digging for a resounding "yes, it's safe," but I couldn't lie, and truth be told, the collapsed tunnels and gaping hole might not be entirely safe.

Regardless of his reservations, he followed me to the rear of the town hall. I'd wanted to go down into the tunnels again, only this time I wanted Levi with me, to try and use his magic to zero in on who or what was down there. For despite all the distractions, there was still a soul stealer who was one soul away from taking up permanent residence in this realm, and that spelled disaster.

The kitchen was as I'd left it. No one had been here since. The pantry doors were wide open, debris scattered on the floor.

"Oops," I muttered, eyeing the mess, "I forgot to clean that up. Come on, let's go through, and I'll fix it from the other side."

"The other side?" Worry clouded his voice, and I chuckled.

"The other side of the wall. Not the *other* side."

"Oh. Right." He followed closely behind, stepping gingerly through the debris until we'd stepped through the hole in the wall. With a wave of my hand, the hole repaired itself. We could hear the shelves slamming back into place, followed by the *thud, thud, thud* of various tins and containers of food returning to their rightful place on the shelves.

"Um, Lucy?"

"Yes?"

"How will we get out?"

"I can always bust us out again," I reassured him, "but my immediate plan was to fly out through the massive crater I made last time."

"Why didn't we come in that way?"

"Too many people about. I'm hoping by the time we're done down here, it'll be late, and everyone will have gone home."

"Good point."

I conjured a light ball that levitated in front of us. "Follow where I was," I instructed it, and it began its descent of the staircase. I remembered this part, and it was easy to see my footprints in the thick dust, but once we'd cleared the long straight tunnel and the floor turned to stone and dirt, there was no trace of the route I'd taken. We came to the first cavern, where it branched off, and I commanded the light ball to stop.

"Take my hands. Let's see if we can channel anything or anyone."

Levi stepped forward and clasped both of my hands in his, facing me.

"Are you leading, or am I?" he asked.

"You. Whoever is responsible somehow has me blocked, but if I give your magic a boost, maybe we'll get the answers we're seeking."

"Okay. Close your eyes. Concentrate." I smiled a little, not needing the instructions, but I'd told him to lead, and he was leading. Closing my eyes, I felt his power shift, concentrate around him. I added my own to it, like boosting a television signal. Like a shockwave, his energy shifted out, disappearing through the rock walls, traveling out, out, out. I couldn't feel anything, but Levi suddenly stiffened.

He would have jerked away if I hadn't kept a firm grip on his hands.

"What is it?" I whispered.

"Can't see yet, but there's something." He leaned a little as if trying to peek around a corner, then straightened up again. "I think the soul stealer is here like you suspected. There's a big...cave? It looks more like a cave, not the smooth walls like here. It's massive. In the middle is water. A lake, maybe? And in the middle of that..." He trailed off.

"What? What's in the middle of the lake?" I urged.

"I'm not sure what it is. A giant sphere. It's huge, about the size of my shop and apartment combined, and it's suspended about a foot above the lake, just floating in the air."

"Okaaaay." Weird. I wondered what the sphere was, what it housed, and why it was here.

"It has symbols on it, and they look like they're glowing. It's kinda beautiful."

"Try and push what you see to me." He'd done it before, sent me a vision all the way to Hell; why couldn't he do it standing in front of me holding my hands? Because some asshole was blocking me, I argued with myself, watching as Levi frowned in concentration. But

I got nothing, not even a flicker of what he was seeing. Okay, I'd have to settle for the next best thing. Releasing his hand, I held out my hand for the light ball, which gently lowered itself until it rested in my palm.

"Place your hand on top of the light," I told Levi, "but keep your focus on what you're seeing."

He squinted open an eye and placed his hand on top of the ball as instructed, then returned his attention to the giant sphere floating above a lake in a massive cavern somewhere beneath Shadow Falls. I turned my attention to the light ball. "Find the location of the sphere, but don't leave yet," I instructed.

The light emanating from the ball dimmed, then brightened several times before it settled.

"Okay, let's go." I let go of Levi's hands, and he snapped open his eyes in surprise.

"What's happening?"

"I'm hoping the light ball managed to zero in on where the sphere is. I connected it to your vision. Now we just need to follow it."

"That's..."

"Cool? Yeah, I know." I grinned, then instructed the light ball to lead the way. It immediately set off across the chamber and down a tunnel. "Slowly!" I called after it, hurrying to catch up before it left us in total darkness.

I didn't know how far we walked or for how long, but my feet and legs were aching. We'd stopped to rest a couple of times, and we'd both taken guesses on where we were in relation to Shadow Falls above us. Nowhere near the town square, that's for sure. We didn't even catch a glimpse of the crater I'd created, and I marveled at who had built these tunnels in the first place and how long it would have taken them.

Eventually, the tunnels changed, the walls becoming jagged and uneven, more like a natural rock formation than man-made. We had to dodge boulders in our path, climbing over or going around, squeezing through narrow openings until finally, we stepped through into the cavern. My mouth dropped open. It was beyond huge. And the lake was more of an ocean, and as Levi had described, hovering over the water was the giant sphere. It was egg-shaped and emitted a white glow, enough to illuminate the cavern. Along the shoreline was black sand broken by a platform of rock that was smooth and flat and had carvings covering it.

"Wow." Levi rested his hand on my shoulder, taking in the magnificence before us. It was breathtaking, that's for sure. "Is this…alien? It looks alien."

"I don't know. Let's find out." If it was alien, I'd have known about it when it arrived on Earth. It would have triggered the alarms in Hell. So how did it get here, and why didn't I know about it? All good questions. Scrambling down the embankment onto the black beach, our boots sank into the sand up to our ankles, making walking difficult. Within seconds I was up to my knees before I realized what it was.

At the same time, I heard Levi saying, "Uh, Lucy?"

"Fuck! It's quicksand!" I cursed, peering over my shoulder to look at Levi, who was sinking fast. *Shit.* Extending my wings, I flapped, pulling myself free, then grabbed Levi's hands and lifted him, flying us both to the stone platform.

"That was unexpected." He puffed, brushing the sand from his pants and shaking his boots.

"A natural phenomenon or a trap?" I wondered.

"Either way, effective."

I crouched, examining the markings on the stone beneath our feet, then glancing at the egg. Same symbols. The symbols on the egg were emitting a faint blue glow. I wondered if it was a language from an ancient time or civilization, but if so, I'd know about it. I knew Earth's history, and while the symbols did look similar to the Egyptian hieroglyphics, there were enough differences to tell me this had nothing to do with the Egyptians. My choices were alien or another dimension. Given we had a creature from another dimension currently running around in this realm, the two had to be related. The question was how. And what was inside the giant egg?

SEVENTEEN

"What do you think it means?" Levi was tracing his fingers over the patterns, following them. "It's like a maze. Each of the symbols has a shallow channel leading to the next one and to the next, and so on. But they all lead here, to the middle, to this stone." He crouched where the channels all led to a white stone embedded in the platform. Placing his palm flat, he lowered his face and squinted along the surface. "I think everything slopes towards the center. Only by a fraction, like a drain."

"So we need liquid to flow through the channels?"

"Could work. What sort of liquid? The water?" He stood with hands-on-hips and looked out at the body of water. It, too, was black like the sand, and I didn't fancy touching it. Who knew what was beneath the surface?

"Let's see." Kneeling on the edge of the platform, he leaned over the edge, cupped his hands, and scooped up the water.

"No, Levi, don't!" But it was too late. I held my breath, but nothing happened. His hands didn't sizzle as if burned by acid as I'd feared. Carefully he poured the water onto the platform, watching as it flowed into the channels and made its way through the maze to the white rock in the center.

"I was right." He grinned triumphantly, and I smiled at his enthusiasm.

"Yeah, but nothing happened. The wrong type of liquid." I hated to burst his bubble but as quickly as the water had flowed through the channels, the quicker it simply evaporated.

"Good observation, sister of mine." The voice behind me was oh so familiar yet not. Gabriel. Spinning on my heel, I faced him.

"Are you responsible for this?" I waved my hand at the egg.

"No hello? No hug for your brother after all this time?" Like me, he hadn't aged. He was still gorgeous to look at with his blonde hair, blue eyes, and golden skin, yet there was something different about him. I could feel it.

"Fine," I huffed, stepping forward. I wrapped my arms around him, felt him do the same, then felt an excruciating pain in my lower back.

"Lucy!" Levi screamed my name, and I staggered back out of Gabriel's embrace to see the glowing sword, once more dripping with my blood. Levi had almost reached me when Gabriel swatted him away as if he were a pesky fly. I turned in time to see him slide on his back across the platform and off the edge into the inky black water.

"Levi!" I rushed to the water's edge, pain slowing me down, and peered into the dark depths. Where was he? Suddenly his head broke the surface, coughing and spluttering. I closed my eyes in a silent prayer of thanks that he was all right. Swimming back to the platform, he heaved himself out of the water.

"Are you okay?" He was by my side in an instant, spinning me, lifting my shirt to examine the wound on my back. It hadn't closed, my blood was running thick and fast, and the pain was disorientating. Like before, I wondered if I was dying.

"Why?" My knees gave out, and Levi lowered me to the ground, holding me close as I glared at my brother, who hadn't moved except to cross his arms over his chest and watch us with interest.

"Always with the questions, Lucy-loo." He sounded so goddamn chirpy I wanted to wipe the smirk right off his face.

"Am I dying?" I asked, for the bleeding wouldn't stop. And then I noticed it. My blood pooling in the channels on the platform, making its way through the maze of symbols toward the center. "Look." I nudged Levi, and he, too, turned his attention to the red pattern my blood had created.

"Relax. You're not going to die." Gabriel shrugged, strolling closer, knowing I was no threat to him while I was bleeding out on the ground.

"Tell me. About the egg. Where did it come from?"

"I suppose it can't hurt to tell you. You're going to find out anyway." Gabriel stopped, watched my blood as it slowly wove its way along the platform. It wasn't moving as quickly as the water had. *Goes to show blood is thicker than water.* "You've had to notice Earth is a mess?" His eyes met mine. "That you're getting more business than us." I nodded slightly. I did agree with his assessment. Earth was out of control, and I'd wondered more than once why Father had let such atrocities happen in this realm.

The way the humans were destroying their own domain and pissing off Mother Nature, who Father had put in charge of the planet itself.

"Through my research, I discovered this"—he nodded at the egg—"in another realm. It has the power to fix everything. So I brought it over—"

"How? How didn't I notice?"

Gabriel laughed. "I told Mother Nature she looked fat; she predictably got mad and triggered an earthquake, and I slipped it through with no one noticing."

"When?"

"Oh, about ten Earth years ago. It needed time to charge."

"Why here? Why Shadow Falls?" Levi asked.

"The veil is thinnest here. It was easier to get it through quickly, unnoticed, and undamaged."

"Why all the tunnels and chambers?"

Gabriel shrugged. "Not my doing. This was already here."

"What does this have to do with the soul stealer? Is the egg from his dimension? Did you do a deal with him?" I could feel the flow of blood was slowing. I was healing. But I didn't move, lay leaning against Levi.

"Always so fucking smart." Gabriel's smile slipped. "That's why he picked you."

"Who?"

"Father. I should be running Hell, not you. It's my right. I was the first. The heir. You stole Hell from me." His words were laced with cold hard fury. Still, he held that against me.

"He chose me. I didn't ask for it," I reminded him.

"You were always his favorite. He made you different, gave you dark hair when the rest of us are light."

"For fuck's sake, Gabriel, get a grip. We all have different hair colors; no two of us are the same. You know that. You're just grasping at straws, trying to find fault so you can continue to hate me when you and I both know you have no reason to."

"Bitch."

"Asshole," I shot back. This reminded me of old times.

Our name-calling drew to a halt when Levi nudged me and whispered, "Look."

My blood had reached the white stone. It pooled under it, then climbed up the sides, defying gravity and completely covering the rock. I watched wide-eyed as the blood sank into the stone and then...

disappeared. The blood that had been weaving its way through the channels was gone, vanished. And the white stone was now...a red crystal. My blood inside it.

"It's time." Gabriel smiled, and I could see his excitement. What the fuck was going to happen now? I was worried. For Levi. For myself. For all of mankind.

A ray of light shot out from the red crystal with an audible click, hitting the egg. I struggled to my feet, Levi supporting me as we watched. The faint blue markings on the egg glowed red, and I couldn't help but shiver at the resemblance to my own magic, for it burned red too. Then the egg slowly began to spin.

"What's happening?" I asked Gabriel, who was practically rubbing his hands together in delight.

"It's working!"

"What's it doing?" I persisted. This couldn't be good.

"It can control time. *I* can control time," he gloated, "and I'm taking Earth back to when it *began* before Father put his precious humans here. The angels will rule this realm."

"What about Heaven? Their home?"

"Heaven is dying."

EIGHTEEN

His comment was offhand, delivered with a shrug, yet his words hit me like a sledgehammer. Heaven was...dying? What the fuck? How? Why? I had so many questions, yet the spinning egg, which was picking up speed and making me nervous, had me keeping my questions to myself. I'd deal with the Heaven situation later.

"Gabriel, you have to stop this. This is insane." I begged, to no avail. And where was Michael in all of this? The two of them had always been as thick as thieves. Why wasn't he here with his brother?

"Lucy?" Levi sounded worried, and I couldn't blame him. The egg was spinning so fast it was a blur. How the Hell did we stop it? My energy was depleted from healing myself, and just like last time I'd been stabbed by the glowing sword, I was feeling tired and woozy.

"Has my wound closed?" I whispered to Levi. He lifted my blood-soaked shirt to look. He nodded. Good. I turned to him, keeping my voice low. "I don't know how we stop this, but my best guess is the red crystal. If we remove it, we might just stand a chance."

"I'll distract him, you get the crystal," Levi whispered, but I shook my head.

"No! He'll kill you. He can't kill me. Even though I'm weak, he can't kill me. I'll distract him. You get the crystal."

"Nice plan, guys, but I've got a better one." Dacian appeared in front of us, the soul stealer in his grip, with Dacian twisting his arm up behind his back. Zuska writhed in agony.

"Do you know what you've done?" I addressed Zuska, who was cursing up a blue streak. "He's not giving you this realm. He's destroying it. He's killing all the souls. There will be nothing here for you. He tricked you."

Noticing our group had grown, Gabriel looked

over before throwing back his head and laughing. "You're fools, all of you!"

"Is this true?" Zuska asked, eyes narrowing.

"That I'm turning back time, ridding the Earth of the *Homo sapiens* species? Correct."

The hum of the egg spinning was getting louder. I figured it was almost at full velocity, and in one fell swoop, the entire human race would be wiped out. We didn't have time to stand around talking.

"How do we stop it?" I snarled at Zuska. "Is it the crystal?"

"Yes, but it's not just the bloodstone. We need power. Lots of it."

"We've got two angels, a psychic, and you. Is that enough?"

He hesitated, then nodded. He was going to help us, of that I was sure, for Gabriel's double-cross meant he had nothing. Still, I had every intention of kicking his ass back to his own dimension once this was done. There would be no more human souls for him.

"Get to the stone. We all need to be touching it at the same time and channel our power into it. Do not break the beam of light to the orb."

"Dacian? Can you help with Gabriel? I was injured...by the sword."

Dacian's eyes met mine, and once again, I caught a glimpse of the friend I used to have. He nodded, then spun and threw a bolt of energy at Gabriel. Gabriel hadn't been paying attention to us. He was fixated on the egg—or orb as Zuska called it—and the blow sent him sliding off the side of the platform and into the quicksand at the far edge.

"Quickly!" We rushed to the red crystal, sliding onto our stomachs, and each of us held out a hand and touched a finger to the red crystal.

"Noooooo!" Gabriel wailed, fighting against the quicksand. We only had a second to get this done before he'd be free.

Closing my eyes, I channeled all of my energy into the crystal, and I felt it—I felt it vibrate beneath my finger. I opened my eyes and looked up. The egg had stopped spinning and was now suffused entirely in red.

"Oh my god, it's going to explode!" As the words left my lips, the egg exploded, the boom deafening, fragments flying through the air, rocks and debris raining down on us, we were flying, twisting, turning, somersaulting through the air. I heard Levi's shout, opened my eyes to try and find him, but we were in some sort of twister, spinning around and around until I grew dizzy and was convinced I was about to throw up.

Then it stopped. I was flung out onto the ground, gravel biting into my cheek as I landed with a thud. *Ouch.* My ears were still ringing, and slowly I pushed myself up. We were in the cemetery on the outskirts of town. How the Hell did we get to the cemetery? Dacian was dusting himself off, stepping from behind a tombstone and apologizing to whoever's grave he'd landed on. Levi was sitting up, running a hand over his face and looking slightly green but otherwise unharmed. Zuska was here too, staggering to his feet.

There was no sign of Gabriel. There was no evidence of what had just happened beneath the Earth. There were just the four of us in the moonlight.

"Is everyone okay?" Dacian asked, coming over and giving me a hand up.

"How did we get here?" Levi asked, looking around.

"It brought me here," Zuska said, walking toward Levi. "This is where I came to this realm. This is where the portal is. It brought me back to it. You were just along for the ride."

"Why?" I asked, puzzled. Dacian and I moved closer to where Levi was standing in front of us.

"It's clear I need to leave this realm. For now." His lips curled, and his smile made my skin crawl. "But I'll be back. With reinforcements." Before I could ask what he meant, the air behind him shimmered, a long slash appearing. He'd opened the portal!

"Levi, step back." But it was too late—the soul stealer wrapped his fingers around Levi's wrist and pulled him through the portal. Levi's startled shout echoed in my ears as I jumped forward, trying to grab his hand, but it was too late. He was through, and the portal closed.

I watched as Levi vanished, a scream I couldn't hear wrenched from my throat. Dacian said something I didn't comprehend. Levi was gone, and I could not wrap my head around it. Any of it. A wave of grief overtook me, and tears fell down my face to splash on my shirt. At that moment, the only thing I could think about was what it would be like to live without Levi. It wasn't a life I wanted. An agony that matched the pain in my back consumed me so fully, I could think of nothing else but the fact that I did not want to go through life without him. My heart contracted so fast, and so strong I felt as if I'd been punched in the chest. I would not survive the force of my pain. I wanted him. I wanted Levi Forrester in my arms, warm, solid, and alive.

Dacian's words dislodged the sobs I was holding onto, and I cried and screamed and railed against him. He pulled me tighter, and I felt genuine empathy radiate off him. No matter that he'd scorned what Levi and I had, I knew he felt remorse. But remorse wouldn't bring Levi back, and the mere thought that I'd lost him was enough to tip me over the edge again.

My screams echoed through the graveyard. No! No, this couldn't have happened. Levi couldn't be taken. He just couldn't. He was mine, and I was his. No matter we belonged to different realms, we would have found a way. If there was one thing I was certain of, it was that.

"Lucy." Dacian was there, holding me in his arms, letting me cry against his chest until eventually, I cried myself out. And that was when it started. The anger. It boiled up from the depths of my soul, bubbling through my veins, consuming me. Thunderclouds tinged with red gathered, red forks of lightning struck the Earth with angry booms. This wasn't over. Not by a long shot.

"Lucy, calm down." Dacian released me, backing away, palms out, a worried expression on his face.

"You're either with me or against me." The rage in my voice changed it. I sounded like a stranger, and I didn't care. I only cared about one thing. Levi. I'd move Heaven and Earth to get him back. And that's precisely what I intend to do.

NINETEEN

The minute a smoking hot angel named Lucifer strolled into my shop, I knew I was in trouble. Not in a sense I would have my ass dragged to Hell and suffer for all eternity trouble. This trouble was centered around my heart—and how it skipped a beat the moment I laid eyes on her, her long black hair swinging around her, not unlike a smoke-filled cloud, giving her an ethereal quality. And her aura. Man, her fucking aura did me in. Like her magic, it was tinged black and red, and it was the most stunning thing— besides her—that I'd ever seen. The darkness around her wasn't evil, though, and I'd initially been surprised. After all, isn't Satan the root of all evil?

But her darkness was sexy and seductive and at the heart of it, filled with good intentions.

All my life, I'd been on the edge, on the outer circle of everyone and everything, talking to the dead tended to ostracize you. I was labeled a fraud, accused of ripping people off, taking their money, and passing on fake messages from the spirit world. The accusations stung, but I couldn't blame anyone for thinking that way because the truth is, the fake psychics are out there, spinning bullshit stories to part you from your hard-earned dollars. Only I'm not one of them. My grandmother had taught me everything I know, not only how to use my skills but how to turn them into a fruitful business. Which I had. I made good money at what I did and had built a reputation for myself—an honorable one. The few girlfriends I'd had never stuck around for long, wanting my undivided attention constantly, which of course, I couldn't do. When the dead wished to speak with you, they weren't going to wait until you'd finished your date.

Until Lucy. Lucy understood the foibles of the dead. Of course, being the devil gave her a distinct advantage in that department. And while I'd never given Heaven or Hell any real thought, of their existence or otherwise, her explanation of the way things were, made perfect sense. I knew there was a veil, that the dead crossed it. Once again, it was only logical that there were other dimensions beyond that veil. She'd opened my eyes to so many possibilities, but what she didn't know, which I did my best to keep from her, was that I knew. I knew the toll her job took on her. I could feel the sadness in her when she slept, tossing and turning at night, her dreams not giving her peace. She didn't enjoy the torture. She wasn't the sadistic bastard everyone thought she was. I snorted. Hell, she wasn't even the male everyone thought Lucifer was.

Lucy cared about others. She seemed to care more about others than she did herself, and that went against everything I thought I knew about Hell. She was different, unique, and I couldn't help the pride that swelled inside me with that knowledge.

I felt her now, slipping away from me and every fiber in every cell of my body screamed in protest. I reached for her, hand extended even as I was propelled backward, jerked off my feet. It all happened so fast yet in slow motion at the same time. The rip in the veil where Zuska had slipped through initially now reopened as he left...taking me with him.

The flash of surprise on Lucy's face, that quickly turned to horror. Her screaming my name and reaching for me, our fingers missing by inches. Then she was gone. I was staring at nothing, dragged backward through a tunnel of wind pushing and buffeting me so I could barely catch a breath. When we finally stopped, I was flung to the ground, and I lay there, gasping, unable to fathom what had happened. I was in another realm, alone. All I could think of was that I needed to get back to Lucy.

"It surprises me you survived the vortex, human," Zuska spoke, reminding me that I wasn't exactly alone. He was responsible for my presence here, wherever here was.

"Oh?" My heart was still thundering in my chest, panic threatening to overwhelm me. I was at his mercy, and that didn't sit well with me.

"None have before you," he admitted, and it became clear why he'd come to Earth. They'd tried stealing humans in the past, and we'd perished during the journey. Leaving them no soul to eat. If you wanted to consume human souls, you had to travel to Earth to do it.

"I wonder if it's anything to do with this?" I asked, holding up the glowing sword that was clenched in my right fist. While my eyes had been on Lucy as I'd been dragged backward, I'd seen Dacian toss me the sword from the corner of my vision, had felt my fingers automatically close around the handle as I'd been jerked back through the portal, and I'd held on with a death grip the entire time. I lay with the sword held up, admiring the glow, wondering how it looked so heavy but felt incredibly light in my grasp.

"How did you get that?" Zuska took a step back, then another. I glanced at him. He was afraid. Of me? Or the sword? I figured it was the sword, but I was the one wielding it, so I let myself take some of the credit. Sufficiently orientated, I swung into a crouching position, eyes on Zuska.

"Send me back," I demanded.

"Can't." Zuska shook his head, backing further away. Launching to my feet, I swung for him, the sword slicing through his shirt, leaving a thin line of blood across his abdomen. Just a scratch, but warning enough. "Send. Me. Back," I repeated.

"I can't," he repeated, clenching his stomach. "I only get one trip, there and back. I've no more power."

I squinted at him, trying to get a sense of what he said was the truth. "You said you were opening the portal, sending for your brethren. You have the power."

"I said I was opening the portal, yes, but I wasn't traveling through it. I was going to summon them." Damn it. Keeping the sword trained on him, I glanced around. This place was desolate, the landscape of rock as far as I could see. Overhead were dark clouds and the constant rumble of thunder—I got the feeling this wasn't a storm rolling in. This was the typical atmosphere for this place. Wherever I was.

"Where are we?"

"My realm."

"I know it's your realm, asshole." My anger moved up a notch. Anger at being taken, not only from my home, my world but Lucy. Her face flashed in my mind again, the sheer terror on her face, the panic as she'd reached for me, the disbelief as the veil closed between us. I could feel her pain, echoing my own in my chest. Whatever our connection was, it was strong. I felt compelled to get back to her. I had to return. Failure was not an option.

"What is this realm called?" I asked again.

"You are in the Broken Forrest." An expression flitted across his face, one I didn't understand. Was it...glee? Even though I'd injured him with the sword, the sorry son of a bitch seemed happy about it. "Why are you smiling?" Now his mouth had twisted into a full-blown smile.

"You spilled my blood." His eyes dropped to where a single drop of blood had fallen onto the stone.

"And?"

"It has alerted my tribe to my return. And that I am hurt."

"They're coming?" I guessed, a feeling of dread settling on my shoulders.

"They are," he agreed, nodding. There was nothing for it. I didn't know how many were coming or what I was up against. The one truth I knew was that they would kill me. They fed on souls, and I'd just presented myself as a very tasty meal. But the only one who knew I was here was standing in front of me. Survival was my only option. Praying for forgiveness, I sprung forward, catching Zuska unaware, wiping the smirk from his face as I plunged the sword through him.

He toppled backward, blood dribbling from his mouth, eyes open, unseeing. Drawing the sword out of his gut, I wiped the bloody blade on his clothing, then bent, checking for a pulse. Dead. I thought I'd be filled with remorse, but strangely enough, I felt empowered. Glancing around, I knew I needed to leave this place before more of his kind arrived. Over to the left was a mass of large rock formations, the only place to hide in this desolate place. I began to jog, hoping I was running away from what was coming and not toward it. And all the while, I thought of Lucy. How the fuck was I going to get back to her? My burning desire to stay alive had little to do with me and all to do with her. She'd awoken in me something I thought I'd never feel, and there was no way I was going to let anyone, soul stealer or not, take that away from me. No one.

Craving more of Lucy and Levi's spellbinding journey? The Devil's Advocate awaits! As the stakes soar higher in this paranormal romance, each choice they make could reshape their destiny.

Grab your copy of The Devil's Advocate here: www.JaneHinchey.com/HellsAngel

Thank you for reading! If you enjoyed this book, I'd greatly appreciate your review.

You can find a complete list of my books, including series and reading order on my website at:

www.JaneHinchey.com

Join my newsletter here:

www.JaneHinchey.com/subscribe

And finally, join my readers group on Facebook here:

www.JaneHinchey.com/LittleDevils

Thank you so much for taking a chance and reading my book . It's readers like you who make this journey worthwhile and fuel my passion for storytelling. Your support means the world to me, and I can't wait to share more exciting stories with you in the future.

xoxo

Jane

FREE BOOK OFFER

Want to get an email alert when a new book is released?

Sign up for my newsletter today,

https://janehinchey.com/subscribe

and as a bonus, receive a FREE e-book of

Cupcakes & Curses!

READ MORE BY JANE

Find them all at www.JaneHinchey.com/books

The Ghost Detective Mysteries

#1 Ghost Mortem

#2 Give up the Ghost

#3 The Ghost is Clear

#4 A Ghost of a Chance

#5 Here Ghost Nothing

#6 Who Ghost There?

#7 Wild Ghost Chase

#8 Easy Come, Easy Ghost

#9 Life Ghost On

Witch Way Paranormal Cozy Mystery Series

#1 Witch Way to Magic & Mayhem

#2 Witch Way to Romance & Ruin

#3 Witch Way Down Under

#4 Witch Way to Beauty & the Beach

#5 Witch Way to Death & Destruction

#6 Witch Way to Secrets & Sorcery

The Gravestone Mysteries

#1 Fur the Hex of it

#2 Battle of the Hexes

#3 What the Hex

The Midnight Chronicles

#1 One Minute to Midnight

#2 Two Minutes Past Midnight

#3 Third Strike of Midnight

Clean Scene Inc.

#1 All in Vein

PARANORMAL ROMANCE/URBAN FANTASY

The Awakening Trilogy

Hell's Angel Trilogy

The Enforcer Series (4 books)

Standalones

Returned

Secret Fates

Destiny's Touch

Blood Cursed

Heart of Darkness

About Jane

Hi there! I'm Jane, crafting tales of paranormal cozy mysteries sprinkled with urban fantasy romance. Between sips of coffee and dodging my mischievous cats, I immerse myself in stories where magic meets everyday life.

Once known as Zahra Stone in the world of steamy urban fantasy, I've now merged those fiery tales under the Jane Hinchey banner. Off the page you'll find me binging on true crime documentaries or sneaking in a power nap. Dive into my stories and join me on an enchanting journey!

Find me here: www.janehinchey.com

facebook.com/janehincheyauthor

instagram.com/janehincheyauthor

amazon.com/Jane-Hinchey/e/B0193449MI

bookbub.com/authors/jane-hinchey

goodreads.com/jane_hinchey

www.ingramcontent.com/pod-product-compliance
Lightning Source LLC
Chambersburg PA
CBHW051305210726

48287CB00002B/669